Buckle for Dust

C000002217

Buckle for Dust and **Theatre503** present

Cotton Wool

by Ali Taylor

UK premiere at Theatre503, London, on 1 April 2008

Cotton Wool
by Ali Taylor

Cast

CALLUM	Joseph Arkley
GUSSIE	Owen Whitelaw
HARRIET	Victoria Bavister
WOMAN	Catherine Cayman

Director	Lisa Spirling
Designer	Polly Sullivan
Producer	Claire Birch
Lighting Designer	Tim Mascall
Composer & Sound Designer	James Drew
Assistant Director	Dan Coleman
Production Manager	Thom Cornall
Stage Manager	Eleanor Bailey

Cotton Wool was created on the Jerwood Arvon Young Playwrights' Apprenticeship 2004/5 and developed at the National Theatre Studio. It received its European premiere at Staatsschauspiel Dresden on 18 January 2008.

The Company

Ali Taylor (Writer)

Theatre credits include: *Porcelain* (Royal Court Jerwood Theatre Upstairs, Workers Writes Festival); *America Street* (Paines Plough Wild Lunch, Young Vic); *November* (Union Theatre/Box of Tricks). Ali was a delegate at Interplay Europe 2002, an international festival for young playwrights in Hungary and tutor at Interplay Europe 2004 in Athens. Radio includes: *Eight Feet High & Rising* (BBC Radio 4).

Joseph Arkley (*Callum*)

Joseph trained at the Royal Scottish Academy of Music and Drama. In 2006 he was awarded the Laurence Olivier Bursary. Theatre credits include: Tom Wingfield in *The Glass Menagerie* (Royal Lyceum Edinburgh); Dim in *Stoopud Fucken Animals* (Loose Collective/Traverse Theatre Company); Lloyd in *Mud* (Gate); Jake in *Moonlight* (Arches Theatre Company). Radio credits include: *Fortunes of War, Dombey and Son, Heart of Midlothian, Resurrection, Beyond the Thunderclouds* (all BBC Radio 4).

Victoria Bavister (*Harriet*)

Victoria graduated from the Oxford School of Drama in 2006. Since leaving she has continued her training at the Caravanserai Acting Studio. Theatre credits include: *Oleanna* (Pentameters Theatre/Caravanserai Productions); *Blasted* (Theatre North national tour); *Kasimir & Karoline* (BAC); *Into the Woods* (The Theatre, Chipping Norton); *Our Town* (Pegasus Theatre); *Blue Remembered Hills* (Ctoo Venue/Rep Theatre Company). TV credits include: *Waking the Dead, Casualty*. Short film credits include: *After the Lunch* (michaelgraham films); *Pure No More* (HJ Films).

Owen Whitelaw (*Gussie*)

Owen is originally from the south east of Scotland and is in his final year at the Royal Scottish Academy of Music and Drama. Theatre credits include: *Rupture* (National Theatre of Scotland); *Spangle Baby, Poorboy, Macbeth, Frantic Red Head, Hidden, Vanishing Point, Cinderella, Women Beware Women, Benny Lynch* (all RSAMD). Radio credits include: *Blindness* (BBC Radio 3); *Acting Up* (BBC Radio Scotland). Short film credits include: *Score*.

Lisa Spirling (Director)

Lisa trained at Royal Holloway University of London, LAMDA and the National Theatre Studio. Theatre credits as director include: *Idiots of Ants* (Pleasance, Edinburgh); *Beowulf* (Storm on the Lawn/Theatre Royal Bath); *Blood Wedding* and *Six Characters in Search of an Author* (Year Out Drama Company); *Can't Stand Me Now* (rehearsed reading, Royal Court); *Beauty and the Beast* (Jacksons Lane); *Driving Miss Daisy, The Hate Plays* (Box Clever); *1001 Nights Now* (British Museum); *This is Your Captain Speaking* (Pentameters Theatre); *Sixteen Sonorous Stones* (Bridewell); *The Vagina Monologues* (Pleasance, London); *The Lying Kind, Oleanna* (LAMDA); *No One Move* (Barons Court); *Gas & Air, New York Threesome* (Edinburgh Fringe & Pleasance, London). Theatre credits as assistant director include: *The Daughter* (The Wedding Collective); *1001 Nights Now* (Northern Stage regional tour); *24 Hour Plays* (Old Vic); *The Little Tempest* (NT Education). Lisa is the artistic assistant at Theatre503 and artistic director for Buckle For Dust.

Catherine Cayman (*Woman*)

Catherine made her West End debut at the Jermyn Street Theatre with *89cc*. Theatre credits include: Imogen in *Cleo, Camping, Emmanuelle and Dick*; Celia in *The Philanthropist*; Beatrice in *The Servant of Two Masters*; Kitty Malone in *Mackey's Lounge*. She has recently toured nationally in Roald Dahl's *The Witches*; Terry Johnson's *Dead Funny*; Louise Roche's *Girls Behind*. Catherine was a soloist for the Royal Fusiliers Concert at the Tower of London, and has also appeared in the West End Festival of Performance.

Polly Sullivan (Designer)

Polly studied sculpture before embarking on the Theatre Design course at Wimbledon, graduating in 2003 with first class honors. Recent designs for theatre include: *A Christmas Carol* (Chickenshed); *Flightpath* (Out of Joint); *Called to Account* (Tricycle); *The Atheist* (Theatre503); *The Snow Dragon* (Soho). Polly has also worked at LAMDA and Oxford School of Drama.

Claire Birch (Producer)

Claire produced the sell-out Royal Court Young Writers Festival 2006/07, including two productions and eight readings. In March 2007 she produced *Breakfast Hearts* and *Choirplay* for Tickle Theatre Company at Theatre503. As an assistant producer for London Artists Projects she worked on a wide range of arts projects and productions, including the opera *Elephant and Castle* at the Aldeburgh Festival 2007. Claire is a freelance producer and arts administrator.

Tim Mascall (Lighting Designer)

Theatre credits include: *Why The Whales Came* (Comedy Theatre); *The Vagina Monologues* (Wyndams); *Lies Have Been Told* (Trafalgar Studios); *Derren Brown – An Evening of Wonder* (Old Vic); *Professor Bernhardi and Rose Bernd* (OSC/Dumbfounded) and *Jenufa* (Natural Perspective Theatre Company) (both at the Arcola); *Vote Dizzy* (Soho); *Road To Nirvana* (Kings Head); *Breakfast With Jonny Wilkinson* (Menier Chocolate Factory); *The Lady Of Burma* (Riverside Studios); *Marilyn and Ella* (Theatre Royal, Stratford East). UK Touring productions include: *Pete and Dud: Come Again*; *The Alchemist*; *Trainspotting*; *Gizmo Love* and *Bad Jazz* (both for Actors Touring Company); *Derren Brown Live 2006, 2007* and *2008*. Other UK productions include: *A Small Family Business* (Watford Palace); *Teenage Kicks* (Mark Goucher Ltd).

James Drew (Composer & Sound Designer)

Recent theatre credits as sound designer include: *Beauty Queen of Leenene* and *Top Girls* (Watford Palace and national tour). As assistant sound designer: *Never Forget Churchill* (Bromley ATG). Keyboard programming: *Fiddler on the Roof* (UK Productions regional tour); *Mamma Mia* (International Productions); *Acorn Antiques* (Phil McIntyre national tour). Production sound: *Into the Woods* (Royal Opera House tour). James is very much looking forward to working with Buckle for Dust.

Dan Coleman (Assistant Director)

Dan is currently the Resident Assistant Director at Theatre503. Assistant Director credits include: *The Final Shot* by Ben Ellis, directed by Tim Roseman (Theatre503); *They Have Oak Trees in North Carolina* by Sarah Wooley, directed by Paul Robinson (Tristan Bates); *The Miser* directed by Philip Hedley (Cochrane). Dan has directed productions at the Bloomsbury Theatre, the Rosemary Branch and the Edinburge Fringe, and is a visiting lecturer at Middlesex University, teaching directing skills and performance theory.

Thom Cornall (Production Manager)

Thom has been a theatre technician since he graduated from Chester University in 2003, where he studied Media for Performance. Thom has worked in a number of different venues, both large and small, and has experience in a variety of disciplines. Since 2006, Thom has been a member of the Bloomsbury Theatre's technical department. *Cotton Wool* is Thom's first show as Production Manager and he is very much looking forward to working with Buckle for Dust.

Eleanor Bailey (Stage Manager)

Eleanor is currently midway through a BA Hons in Stage Management at Rose Bruford College. Recent stage management credits include: *The Gondoliers* (Greenwich); *I am a Superhero* (Theatre503).

Buckle for Dust

Buckle for Dust

Buckle for Dust is a collective of playwrights, directors and producers dedicated to telling stories.

We believe stories for the stage should be imaginative, metaphorical and visually brilliant. We have a passion for new plays with a twisted take on the everyday world.

Buckle for Dust fights to create opportunities for distinctive voices.

We are:

Claire Birch
Michael Camp
Nancy Harris
Lou Ramsden
Juliette Oakshett
Lisa Spirling
Ali Taylor

For more information on the company please see our website: **www.bucklefordust.org.uk**, or email us at **info@bucklefordust.org.uk**

Buckle for Dust would like to thank the following for their support:

Theatre503, The Rod Hall Agency, The Daily Record, The Latchmere, Out of Joint, Jacksons Lane, Royal Court Theatre Young Writers' Programme, ASA, Arvon Foundation, National Theatre Studio, Fish Productions, Radford Wallis, Peggy Ramsay Foundation, Oppenheim-John Downes Memorial Trust, Arts Council South East, Bar 333, Macdonald and Taylor Ltd, AG Barr, The Ambassador Theatre Group.

Charlotte Knight, Ola Animashawun, Meredith Oakes, David Eldridge, Natalie Davies, Brian Edwards, Matt Deegan, Joe Atkins, Alex Woolnough, Tara Siddall, Kathryn Jein, James Anthony Pearson, Chris Adlington, Mercy Ojelade, Katerina Zaripova.

All our friends and families and all the supporters whose generosity made this production possible.

Theatre503

Theatre503 is the home of fearless, irreverent, brave and provocative new plays. Under the direction of Tim Roseman and Paul Robinson, it aims to be a crucible where writers, directors, actors and designers can develop their skills and vision while producing the highest quality work.

The theatre has played host to some of the most exciting writers of their generation, including Dennis Kelly, Duncan Macmillan and Rachel Wagstaff. It has won the Peter Brook Empty Space Award, was nominated in 2006 for a Time Out Live Award and was recently ranked alongside the National, the Royal Court, Soho and The Bush as one of *Time Out*'s top five new writing venues.

503 receives no national subsidy and is therefore indebted to those individuals whose generous donations keep the theatre afloat (to learn about its Friends programme, email **development@theatre503.com**) – as well as to the team of experienced and dedicated volunteers, without whose time, energy and imagination nothing that 503 achieves would be possible.

Artistic Directors	**Tim Roseman & Paul Robinson**
General Manager	**Ed Errington**
Programming Director	**Gene David Kirk**
Literary Manager	**Sarah Dickenson**
Literary Co-ordinator	**Steve Harper**
Senior Reader	**Will Hammond**
Press Consultant	**Lyndsay Roberts**
Press Co-ordinator	**Tom Atkins**
Marketing Co-ordinator	**Antonio Ferrara**
Front of House Manager	**Sarah Beck**
Education Directors	**Anthony Biggs & Jessica Beck**
Development Co-ordinator	**Jennie Cashman**
Business Development	**Barbara Chiodo**
Casting Directors	**John Manning & Annelie Powell**
Resident Assistant Director	**Dan Coleman**

Theatre503, The Latchmere
503 Battersea Park Road, London SW11 3BW

Charity No. 1115555 I Company No. 5694721

COTTON WOOL

Ali Taylor

For Lou

Characters

CALLUM, *eighteen*
GUSSIE, *sixteen*
HARRIET, *seventeen*
WOMAN

Dialogue in [ ] is intention, not to be spoken.

A forward slash (/) in the text indicates the point at which the next speaker interrupts.

This text went to press before the end of rehearsals and so may differ slightly from the play as performed.

Scene One

Darkness. A deserted beach in Kirkcaldy, Scotland. It is December and the wind is blustery, bitter and cold.

GUSSIE *and* CALLUM *fall from above, over the sea wall and onto the beach, shouting in delight. They have been sprinting and are out of breath. Both are dressed in scruffy dark suits, white shirts and black ties, scruffy trainers.* GUSSIE *has a carrier bag full of cans of lager.* CALLUM *carries a bottle of cheap vodka and a bottle of Pernod.*

GUSSIE. Did ye see me, man; were ye lookin'?

CALLUM. The whole way!

GUSSIE. Three fences, gardens, bins, bushes, doon the alley and over tha' wall and down, ay –

CALLUM. The pavements licked up behind ye –

GUSSIE. Pounding the streets –

CALLUM. Like a fuckin' sprinter.

GUSSIE. High-jumper!

CALLUM. Pole-vaulter!

GUSSIE. Brand new, man, brand fuckin' new.

Puggled ye are now, eh?! Bet ye fuckin' are.

CALLUM. Havenae run so fast in ma life. I thought ma lungs were gonna burst like balloons.

GUSSIE. See, you should lose a few o' thae pounds, big man. Wanna be trim like me. No' an ounce of lard on us.

CALLUM. Jesus, am gonnae chuck. Aye, I am. Am gonnae chuck.

CALLUM *bends over and prepares to be sick.* GUSSIE *puts the carrier bag down. He takes out a can of strong lager and opens it. It fizzes over the top.* GUSSIE *catches the froth with his mouth.* CALLUM *is sick.*

GUSSIE. You should harden yerself up like me. I can run all night when I'm pished. You're gettin' old. It's all downhill from eighteen.

GUSSIE *walks to the edge of the surf.*

Fuckin' dark here, man.

This definitely the right beach?

CALLUM. Aye, course.

GUSSIE (*shouts*). Hullo? Hullo?

Anybody there?

CALLUM *stands and wipes his mouth with his sleeve.*

CALLUM. S'all ours, bro.

GUSSIE. Brand new. What we got here then?

GUSSIE *takes a second can out of the bag and throws it to* CALLUM.

Nice one.

CALLUM. Dunno if I can, Gussie.

GUSSIE. U-huh, no way José. Get it doon ye. Ye're no' here for the bracing sea air.

CALLUM *opens the can. It fizzes and spills down his jacket.*

CALLUM. Ah shite.

CALLUM *takes a swig of lager, swills it around his mouth and spits it out. He then finishes the rest of the can in one long gulp. He takes another can from the bag and opens it.*

Cheers.

GUSSIE. Aye, cheers, bro.

CALLUM. Here's tae the worst fuckin' day of our life.

They clink cans and drink.

GUSSIE. But we're no' rememberin' it.

CALLUM. No' a word.

GUSSIE. Or a thing.

Just getting battered.

CALLUM. Steamin'.

GUSSIE. Aye, steamin'. Like a steamy bath full of steam.

CALLUM. And Stella.

GUSSIE. Aye, steam and Stella.

CALLUM. Cheers.

GUSSIE. Cheers.

They clink cans and drink.

You properly sure about this place? Fuckin' spooky. All they trees back there. Bet they're full o' witches.

CALLUM. Aye, c'mon. Get that doon ye.

CALLUM *opens the bottle of vodka and takes a swig.*

GUSSIE. Am impressed wi' you, by the way. You know this is private property? Sign up there says it's a private beach. Wi' us wheakin' these cans, this the second criminal act you've committed in half an hour. Ye all right wi' that?

CALLUM. You serious? Is it?

GUSSIE. Aye. A private beach. It means you're a trespasser.

CALLUM. Oh no, Gussie.

CALLUM *stops drinking, worried.*

GUSSIE. C'mon, ya dick. It's no' as if the polis patrol down here. Kirkcaldy's no' exactly *Baywatch.* Pamela Anderson's no' gonna be jogging doon here... unless she wants dysentery.

CALLUM *drinks.*

That's more like it, bro. Cheers.

CALLUM. Aye, cheers.

They clink cans and drink. GUSSIE *throws a pebble into the sea. Beat.*

Gussie?

Gussie?

Think any thae wankers minded?

GUSSIE. When?

CALLUM. This afternoon. You know, us sneakin' out.

GUSSIE. Ach, tell ye, fuck 'em, Callum. Where were they the last six months? No' a cheep till the news is oot. Then, suddenly they're round us like flies round shit. Most of them only there today for free cheese-on-sticks. Mind Auntie Jude, 'Lovely day for it.' 'The sun's out, she must be watchin'.'

Up their arses, man.

CALLUM. Uncle Bill.

GUSSIE. Pishheed.

CALLUM. Gave us this.

CALLUM takes £100 out of his pocket.

GUSSIE. Christ! Straight up? No' so bad him then.

CALLUM. Telt us, 'Take it and fuck off.'

GUSSIE. Prick.

Pause.

I didnae ken any o' they hymns, Callum. Felt like a right fanny, mouthin' along.

CALLUM. How'd all that Jesus shit get intae the service? It's no' as if I asked for it.

GUSSIE. Wasnae me. That vicar talkin' as if he knew her when he'd never set eyes on her in his life. Hymns wi' nae relevance. Everyone nodding like he talking the truth.

Best out of it.

CALLUM. Aye. Bastards the lot o' them.

CALLUM stands.

(*Shouts, holding his can aloft.*) Cheers, ye fuckers. Ye've been shite tae us but… nae more, eh.

Beat.

What?

GUSSIE. Nothing.

CALLUM. C'mon, what?

GUSSIE. Tell ye, I've got the heebie-jeebies.

CALLUM. Have a drink, wee man. We've all those tae get through.

GUSSIE. Am no' jokin'. Shivers. All the way up here. It's like
goose pimples or that. There's something wrong about this
place.

CALLUM. Aye, murderers everywhere.

GUSSIE. Shut up!

CALLUM. Might be. Imagine gettin' lost out here. Among the dark
trees. Trying to get home but the roots catchin' yer feet and
leaves ticklin' yer cheeks. Lost and trapped, till the fairies find
ye... And ye ken whit the fairies do...

GUSSIE. Shut up, Callum!

Slight pause. GUSSIE *stands and looks inland.*

Tell ye, there's someone watchin' us, bro. I swear. I always get the
shivers when I'm bein' watched. I've got them right down my –

CALLUM. Gussie!

GUSSIE. I swear. There's something.

Can you see anything?

CALLUM. There's nothing there.

GUSSIE. I got a sixth sense.

CALLUM. No sense.

He looks around again and then sits.

GUSSIE. Am no' fuckin' jokin'. I have got sense, by the way. Just
cos you got a Higher, think you're Einstein.

Pause.

About time to go, eh?

CALLUM. Got six cans left. Gussie, this is supposed to be a
memorial drink. Our memorial drink. This, Gussie... (*Holding
up his can.*) This one's for Mammy.

Gussie?

7

GUSSIE. It's freezin'. Socks are soakin', I cannae feel my toes.

CALLUM. 'You wanna build yersel' up, man. Be a bit more like me. When I'm pished, I could do this all night.'

GUSSIE. Funny. Billy fuckin' Connolly, you.

GUSSIE *looks around furtively.* CALLUM *walks to the surf.* GUSSIE *walks to the bag, picks up the bottles of spirits and puts them in the bag.*

CALLUM. You know, I mind comin' doon tae this beach wi' Mammy. Musta been about six or that. It was summer but as cold as noo. Windy too. Couldnae afford a bucket and spade so I had a cup and spoon. Just spent the whole day diggin' down, wee tunnels, waitin' till they filled up wi' water. Mammy watchin', wi' you runnin' around eatin' sand.

She said if I kept goin' I'd get to Australia.

I said I didnae want to, cos I liked where we were, things as they were.

CALLUM *notices something out at sea and stares at it.*

GUSSIE. Very nice. See me, am oo-ay here.

If it's five miles back, I better get started. Christ, I hate having wet toes.

Pause.

Callum.

Callum?

CALLUM. Sshh. Shut up. Dinnae move. You still got the shivers, wee man?

CALLUM *walks to the edge of the surf.* GUSSIE *looks over to* CALLUM. CALLUM *is stood frozen to the spot.*

GUSSIE. Callum?

What?

CALLUM. Nothing. C'mon, Gussie, we're going.

GUSSIE. What ye lookin' at? That's the sea, ye twat.

CALLUM. Forget it. Grab the bottles. C'mon.

GUSSIE. No' unless ye tell us what you're / looking at.

CALLUM *points out to sea.*

CALLUM. There.

GUSSIE *looks, straining.*

In the moonlight.

CALLUM *looks out to the object in the sea. He is clearly distressed.*

GUSSIE. What is it?

What the…? Looks like –

(*Shaking his head.*)… Jesus.

What we gonna dae?

CALLUM. Dunno.

GUSSIE *picks up a stone and throws it at the object.*

What ye daein'?

GUSSIE. You got a better idea?

(*Shouts.*) Hey! Hey!

How long's it been there?

CALLUM. Just noticed.

GUSSIE *takes off his jacket and runs up to his knees in the water.*

No, Gussie!

GUSSIE. Am goin' in.

Might still be –

I told yer, man, there was something.

CALLUM. No way.

GUSSIE. Oh Jesus fuck.

Pause.

CALLUM. Don't move. It might float in.

GUSSIE. You know what it looks like!?

9

CALLUM. No.

GUSSIE. You know what it fuckin' looks like?

CALLUM. It's no' what you think!

GUSSIE. Then what the hell is it, Callum?!

What the hell is it?!

Scene Two

Later that night. A bedroom in the boys' house. It is impoverished. The carpet is rolled up to one side, filthy. The floorboards are bare and covered with clothes, litter, half-filled cereal bowls, cups, etc. There is a pile of sealed boxes piled up in one corner of the room. There are two lilos on the floor with sleeping bags and dirty duvets on them. CALLUM's is neat and tidy. GUSSIE's is unmade and has underwear and litter all over it. A single electric radiator is plugged into one wall next to CALLUM's bed.

CALLUM, still in his suit, unzips a large tatty suitcase. GUSSIE stands, also still in his suit, on the other side of the room. He is out of breath from running and staring angrily at CALLUM.

GUSSIE. Thanks a fuckin' lot, mate. Where did you go so quick? Ran off wi' a banger up yer arse.

CALLUM. Take this.

CALLUM pushes the smaller bag from inside the suitcase into GUSSIE's arms. CALLUM takes off his jacket.

GUSSIE. Why did ye leave me there, eh? I've spent three hours gettin' back here, ye cunt. Beltin' doon out there, by the way. Am drookit.

CALLUM. Get the jersey, wee man. In the bag.

Hurry up, we no' got time.

GUSSIE. For what?

CALLUM. Gi' us the jersey. And they shirts and trousers. I want them folded. Them *(Re: some socks.)* picked up and in there. *(Re: the bag.)*

GUSSIE *picks up the jumper but doesn't pass it to* CALLUM.

GUSSIE. Callum, hang on a wee moment. Whit ye doin'?

CALLUM. We're packin' up. We're leavin'.

CALLUM *picks up clothes and belongings scattered across the floor. He puts them into the suitcase.*

You want tae leave, Gussie. Said ye did. On the beach, ye said ye wanted to leave.

GUSSIE. When did I?

CALLUM. There's nae point hangin' around.

GUSSIE. Wait a minute. When did I say I wanna leave?

CALLUM *pushes past* GUSSIE *and rolls up his bedding.* CALLUM *busily continues to throw things towards the open bag. He turns the electric radiator off at the socket.*

CALLUM. That in there, that in there. The rest is going in that one. There's a train tae Edinburgh at 6.14; the first one. That's two hours. We'll get that. Third platform. Then London.

Mind ye pilly.

GUSSIE. I dinnae gi' a shite about me pilly –

CALLUM. Half-hour tae Edinburgh, then five hours down. Dave's mate Gary's in Dalston, we'll kip at his.

GUSSIE. Callum, for fuck's sake!

Wait.

Stop.

Stop.

What did we just fuckin' see?

Beat.

CALLUM. There wasnae anythin'. It was the moonlight.

GUSSIE. Ah, fuck off. Am no' goin' blind yet. I saw it as clear as fuckin' day.

CALLUM. Ye're pished. Trick o' the light. It was a piece of wood, or buoy or a something.

11

We dinnae need this now. We've had enough go wrong already.

GUSSIE *turns the electric radiator on at the socket and then faces* CALLUM *and shakes.*

GUSSIE. Am dryin' my socks.

GUSSIE *sits, takes his shoes and socks off and hangs a sock over the radiator.*

CALLUM. No' there, Gussie. On your side at least.

GUSSIE. Got a better idea? Dinnae remember the rest of the house havin' any heatin', man.

GUSSIE *lays the other sock on the radiator.*

This is typical you, eh? Doin' yer big-brother thing. 'I know what's best. Leave it tae me. I'll decide.' Am here too, mind.

CALLUM *continues to pack.* GUSSIE *gets changed into jeans, T-shirt and trainers.*

Been a perfect day, ent it? No' even pished any more.

Beat.

I saw hair, Callum.

I saw her hair fannin' out in the water.

I saw her white arms. Stretched out.

I know you saw.

Slight pause.

CALLUM. What ye wanna do about it, Gussie?

GUSSIE. I dunno. Polis at least.

CALLUM. That a good idea, is it, genius?

GUSSIE. They'll be some lassie missin'. Folk'll be out looking for her.

CALLUM. Aye, they might. And you'll tell 'em where you saw her.

GUSSIE. Why not?

CALLUM. And tell the bizzies you were trespassin' on a private beach, with a load of booze ye'd wheaked.

GUSSIE. Why the fuck would I tell them that?

CALLUM. They'll wanna know. Why you were there, what you were doin', why you had it, why did ye come back to yer house, why did ye no' report it earlier? And while we're at it, where's yer mammy? Oh, sorry, lads. Pa no' around? Then why you two livin' on your tod? For how long you been? Ah hospice? Are you no' sixteen? Should yer no' be wi' social services in a care home?

Forget it. We're getting the train oo-ay here.

Pause.

Do you no' want shot of it? You see the way folk look at us; starin' as if we're scum.

GUSSIE. We are scum. Pure Fifer scum. They stare cos we're different. Folks scared of what they don't understand.

You should be proud o' it.

CALLUM. No, Gussie, I'm sick o' it.

We cannae stay here. I want something special oo-ay life. I want money and mates and a bit of a laugh. I willnae get it here. This is the end of the world.

GUSSIE. No, it's no'.

CALLUM. Well, I'd like tae fuckin' see it then.

GUSSIE. But it's home, Callum.

CALLUM. We've buried our home. This is Mammy's house got wi' Mammy's money and wi' all Mammy's things. It's no' ours.

GUSSIE. I grew up here.

CALLUM. Aye, as a family. The three of us in the whole house. Nae living with a poxy heater in one room wi' no gas, no fuckin' heating. It's no' a home any more. It's a shell wi' us in it.

CALLUM *continues to pack.* GUSSIE *moves towards the boxes.*

Giz a hand packin' up.

No' them. They're stayin' here.

GUSSIE. We gottae.

CALLUM. I'll come up and get 'em when we're settled.

GUSSIE. But they're… What if they, you know, we'ans break in.

CALLUM. They'll go in the loft then.

GUSSIE. We gotta take these, man. Mammy's things, Callum.

Pause.

I'm no' leavin' them. If they're no' goin' I'll stay here.

CALLUM. We're no' takin' them.

GUSSIE. Then am no' budgin'.

CALLUM. Gussie, we dinnae need they things any more.

GUSSIE *rips a piece of Sellotape off one box and takes out a scarf. He scrunches it up, smells it and puts it in his bag.*
CALLUM *changes into jeans and a T-shirt. He then lies down on the floor. He pulls a pillow under his head.*

Get some kip, Gussie. At six o'clock, we're leavin'.

Scene Three

The next day. Dawn. GUSSIE *on the top of a cliff overlooking the beach. Dawn.* GUSSIE *is dressed in two jumpers, tracksuit bottoms and trainers. He looks out to sea. Although it is no longer raining, he is soaking wet. He is twitchy and furtive. He eats a shop-made sandwich from a plastic bag full of ready-made sandwiches next to him.*

He takes CALLUM's *notebook out of his pocket. He notes something in the book and then lays it carefully on the ground. He lays the pen carefully parallel to the notebook.*

Enter CALLUM, *dressed in tracksuit bottoms and trainers and also wearing a waterproof cagoule. He sits next to* GUSSIE.

CALLUM. 6 a.m., ye wee twat.

GUSSIE. I know.

CALLUM *watches as* GUSSIE *gazes out to sea.*

What? You've got your 'I've just missed *Star Trek*' face on.

CALLUM. The train's gone too –

GUSSIE. Has it – ?

CALLUM. You know it has. Have I no' been lookin' for you? I was fuckin' [worried] …

GUSSIE. What?

CALLUM. Nothing.

Whit ye daein' wi' ma wee book? Gettin' it wet.

GUSSIE *snatches the book from the ground.*

You take it last night?

GUSSIE. Ye didnae notice a thing, head back, snorin' like pig on heat. You're too easy tae pinch stuff off. You're fuckin' naïve, boy.

CALLUM. Big word for you, Dumbo. Only thing I am is stupid enough to trust you. Thought we'd sort ourselves together.

GUSSIE. Aye, but no' on an empty stomach, eh. Take it easy.

Want a piece?

GUSSIE *opens up the plastic bag full of sandwiches.*

CALLUM. Where'd you get they from?

GUSSIE. Garage.

CALLUM. Pay?

GUSSIE. Course.

CALLUM. What with?

GUSSIE. My charm, man. The old biddies in there love it. Wee bit o' tho Sean Connery and they're wettin' their tummy huggers. (*He does a Sean Connery impression.*) 'This shandwich ish especially delishious-looking, mishus. I'll take it for free. Thanksh. Oh, sixsh? You're too kind.'

CALLUM *takes a sandwich.*

No' the meat ones.

CALLUM. Cheese all right?

GUSSIE *nods and takes a sandwich himself.*

GUSSIE. As many o' they shitey fishy ones as ye like.

CALLUM. You gonna tell us whit ye're doin' here?

GUSSIE. Observin'.

GUSSIE *holds up the book.* CALLUM *tries to take it from him.*

CALLUM. Giz it.

GUSSIE. No way. Am no' havin' you takin' over. This is mine, this.

CALLUM. I won't. Giz it.

GUSSIE. Promise. Cross yer heart and hope tae… just cross yer heart.

Pause. CALLUM *reluctantly crosses his heart.*

CALLUM. I'll. No'. Take. Over.

GUSSIE *hands* CALLUM *the book.* CALLUM *wipes the rain off the book. He reads out loud.*

You better no' have written anything stupid in here.

GUSSIE. Don't worry, all your wee notes and numbers are still there.

CALLUM. 'The pier.' What's that, 'Tanker'?

GUSSIE *nods.*

'Beach. Grass. Buoy.'

What's the point o' this?

GUSSIE. Cataloguin'.

CALLUM. Cataloguin'?!

GUSSIE. I know! Am becomin' as nerdy as you. Two hours that's taken me.

GUSSIE *stands and walks to the edge of the cliff.*

I've worked it out. The current, right, runs that way. (*Indicates left to right.*) Last night, we were there. (*Points left.*) Anything in the water will be washed around tae there. (*Points dead ahead.*)

CALLUM. C'mon, Gussie. We were pished. Who knows what was there? Coulda been Nessie or Lord Lucan oot for a dip.

GUSSIE. Are you no' a wee bit curious? You saw, wi' yer own eyes, a body floating in the water. Is it no' pricking your curiosity even a wee bit?

CALLUM. Maybe, a bit –

GUSSIE. Then we're gonna find out.

CALLUM. Find out what, Gussie?

Pause.

GUSSIE. Who she was.

CALLUM. Why, man?

GUSSIE. They'll be someone out there missin' her. They'll wanna know where she ended up. Why she… you know. They'll need tellin' that she's no' coming back.

CALLUM. Dunno, bro.

GUSSIE. C'mon, Callum.

CALLUM. This is no' a… I mean. (*He takes Uncle Bill's money from his pocket.*) See here, this can get us to Edinburgh. At least. Then we could go anywhere. Manchester, London. Me and you could be eating scones wi' Betty and Phil next week, throwin' sticks tae the corgis.

GUSSIE. I will come, man.

CALLUM. Will ye?

GUSSIE. Aye. If we do this first. Agreed?

Pause.

Callum?

CALLUM. A dead bird in the sea. It's fuckin' morbid.

GUSSIE. Maybe I'm in a morbid mood.

CALLUM. If you're gonna dae it, it's gottae be done properly. Giz the book.

GUSSIE *shakes his head, refusing.*

C'mon, ye tit.

GUSSIE *hands* CALLUM *the book. He holds his arm straight out towards the buoy floating in the sea.*

From here, the beach left is zero degrees. That way, (*Straight ahead.*) tae ninety degrees, then west is a hundred-eighty.

(*Hands* GUSSIE *the book.*) Read out what we got so far.

GUSSIE. Affirmative, captain. Tae the east. Ravenscraig.

CALLUM (*looking*). Check. Fifteen degrees.

GUSSIE. Breakwater.

CALLUM. Check.

GUSSIE. The buoy.

CALLUM. A hundred and seventy-five. Check.

GUSSIE. You don't have to say 'check'. You're no' a squaddie.

CALLUM. Hurry up. You wanna note of everythin' out there.

GUSSIE. That tanker. Moving easterly.

CALLUM. Forty-eight degrees. Check.

GUSSIE (*looks disgustedly at* CALLUM). Two more sea buoys, breakwaters, the beach.

That's it.

CALLUM. Aye, no' a pretty picture, is it. Welcome to Scotland.

So she's no' out there then.

CALLUM *continues to look through the binoculars.* GUSSIE *takes a sandwich out of the bag. He throws the sandwich away.*

GUSSIE. Guess no'.

CALLUM. Hey, where ye goin'? Ye wanna find out what we saw?

Gussie, don't ye?

GUSSIE. Ach, what's the point, eh? Ye can see there's fuck all out there.

Musta got pulled around by another current, I dunno.

CALLUM. You have to keep lookin'. It's no' gonna be easy. Might have tae be here for days. See, we could camp out. Wi' a wee fire. Keep watch, like. Make notes of any changes in the vista.

GUSSIE. Feel free, man.

CALLUM. But we'd need binoculars. And a hide. I can get ye a cagoule like this. It'll be like an adventure.

GUSSIE. Sounds top, bro.

Beat. GUSSIE *stands to one side. He looks over the cliff to the sea.* CALLUM *puts the notebook down.* GUSSIE *sits on the cliff edge.*

CALLUM. Watch yersel' –

GUSSIE. There's nothing out there, Callum. It was all in our head, eh?

Must be losin' ma mind, like.

CALLUM *sits next to* GUSSIE.

CALLUM. You're not. It's not gonnae happen. Those days are gone. See you, first sign of any loopy shit and I'll be rid o' yer. Sign ye up for *Big Brother*.

He holds the book out to GUSSIE.

Took over, didn't I?

GUSSIE *doesn't take the book. He notices something on the beach below. He looks down.*

GUSSIE. Aye aye.

CALLUM. What?

GUSSIE. This is something for yer wee book. A proper observation.

A bird, Mr Oddie. And no' the feathery variety.

Scene Four

Moments later. HARRIET *is dressed in a black top, black trousers and a black coat. She sits on the beach below, between a large open suitcase, a holdall and a handbag. It is wet and she has been soaked through. On the top of the clothes packed into the suitcase are letters. She is in the middle of making one of the letters into a paper aeroplane. She finishes it and throws it towards the sea.*

Enter CALLUM *and* GUSSIE, *excited, at speed.*

GUSSIE. Oi!

Oi you, hen.

Ye not seen the tide? It's comin' in.

GUSSIE *crouches next to* HARRIET.

Hen?

HARRIET. I ain't a chicken.

GUSSIE. Whit?

HARRIET. Hen. I ain't a chicken.

GUSSIE. The sea's gonnae be up tae armpits in a couple of minutes.

HARRIET. So what?

GUSSIE. You'll drown, won't ya.

HARRIET. Yeah.

GUSSIE. Why'd you wanna do that? Top-lookin' bird like you.

HARRIET. Forget it. You too young.

GUSSIE. Am sixteen and a very sensitive listener.

CALLUM. So am I. Very sensitive.

GUSSIE. No' as sensitive as / me but –

HARRIET. Whatever. I don't care.

HARRIET *moves her suitcases nearer the surf.*

CALLUM. Hey, that's the water.

HARRIET. Cheers, mate. If there anything else obvious you wanna say...

GUSSIE. Oh Jesus, she's a mental, Callum.

You're no' alone. Most people here are... (*Taps the side of his head.*) One bloke that way, I've seen shoutin' at the waves, tellin' them they're a disappointment. Used to be my teacher.

HARRIET. I ain't mental, all right.

GUSSIE. You a junkie then? We got mates that're junkies. It's no problem.

HARRIET. Why you starin'? I ain't wearing a suit of diamonds.

CALLUM *picks up a plane. As* CALLUM *faces* HARRIET, GUSSIE *picks up a plane.* CALLUM *begins to open up the plane but stops when* HARRIET *reacts.*

CALLUM. What are these?

HARRIET. Leave 'em. Don't touch 'em, they're mine.

GUSSIE. These love letters?

HARRIET. No! Don't read it!

CALLUM. Gussie, no.

GUSSIE. 'Dear Harriet.'

HARRIET. Give 'em here, you prick.

GUSSIE. 'I miss you every day you're not with me. Love D.' Aye aye, Callum. Who's 'D', Harriet? Yer boyfriend? Girlfriend? You a lezza, hen?

CALLUM. Gi' the lady back her letters, Gussie.

HARRIET *picks up the remaining paper aeroplanes and stuffs them into her suitcase.*

HARRIET. It none o' yours. I just come down here to think, not get the nth degree.

GUSSIE. C'mon, I'm just joking.

HARRIET. No, you ent joking cos jokes are funny and you ain't funny.

GUSSIE. Must be a lezza, Callum. That right?

HARRIET. Course I ain't. Now am not talking to you so why don't you and your mate go play on the motorway, yeah.

HARRIET *sits on her suitcase.* GUSSIE *backs off.* CALLUM *squats down next to her on his haunches.* GUSSIE *waits for* HARRIET *to be distracted and swipes her handbag.*

GUSSIE (*muttering*). Fuckin' nuts, worra looney tune, radio rental.

CALLUM. Why you throwing letters into the sea, Harriet?

HARRIET. Cos I don't need 'em any more, they don't mean nothing. They full of promises that weren't kept. Lies, man.

CALLUM. What ye doin' then, Harriet?

HARRIET. Dunno, do I? Maybe I'll just sit on this, smoke fags and wait for tide to carry us out to sea. If this the end of the world, maybe I'll float off it.

GUSSIE. Why'd ye no' come out wi' us? Hit the town. We'll show you the high life of Kirkcaldy.

HARRIET. You're Cub Scouts?

CALLUM. We got a Wetherspoon's. I'm eighteen, his older brother.

GUSSIE. Dinnae look too bad, do we?

HARRIET. Seen worse. I know badder boys than you. You nothin'.

GUSSIE. Bonnie 'n' Clyde, me and him, so.

HARRIET. Who's Bonnie?

GUSSIE. Me obviously. No' gonna be Plug here.

CALLUM. Cheers, Gussie.

GUSSIE. Seen his nose?

CALLUM. Least I'm no' in dresses.

GUSSIE. Nor am I.

CALLUM. Bonnie's a girl, stupid.

GUSSIE. What? Aye, I knew that. Just showin' the lady ma sense of humour.

HARRIET. Ain't you bit skinny for a bad boy?

GUSSIE. No' just bad boys. Show you a good time. What do ye say? Maybe the pier, arcade.

HARRIET. Classy.

GUSSIE. I know.

HARRIET. Throw in a pizza.

GUSSIE. Double cheese, even. He's minted.

CALLUM. Jesus, Gussie!

GUSSIE. Eat it back our house. We got a whole place tae ourselves, hen. No one else around, nae bother.

HARRIET. Ain't your mummy lookin' after ya?

Beat.

GUSSIE. Whit about my mammy?

HARRIET. Easy, Casanova.

CALLUM. Nothin', mate.

GUSSIE. What you fuckin' sayin' about my mammy?

HARRIET. Only sayin'.

GUSSIE. I'm no' havin' her talk about Mammy, Callum.

HARRIET. I didn't mean nothin' by it. So chill, yeah.

CALLUM. Our mammy's no' around, Harriet.

HARRIET. Nor's mine. Guess we the same. Laters.

> HARRIET *grabs her suitcase and holdall and moves away from them, up the steps, off the beach and onto the pavement. The boys stay where they are.*

GUSSIE. Oi! I'm offerin' you pizza. I'm talkin' tae you, ya bitch.

HARRIET. Have you got a problem?

GUSSIE. Only wi' your face.

CALLUM. Gussie, chill out, man.

GUSSIE. We come down here special. No' likin' gettin' attitude.

HARRIET. I'm giving you attitude?

GUSSIE. Aye. We're here to be nice, to say hello, to make ourselves known to you. Being a new bird, thought you'd like to… friends, you know.

HARRIET. That right?

CALLUM. Aye. We're being friendly.

GUSSIE. But if you no' like it, you can get to fuck. We're no' fuckin' desperate.

HARRIET. I thought you were being friendly.

CALLUM. We are.

HARRIET. Sounds like something else.

GUSSIE. You can dream. I wouldn't touch you with his.

HARRIET moves and gets to the exit.

CALLUM. Hey.

HARRIET. What?

CALLUM. Don't go. Yer planes.

GUSSIE. I've got a question. You're fucking ugly. Are you a vampire?

HARRIET exits, with her suitcase and bag.

Scene Five

Later that day. CALLUM *and* GUSSIE *are sitting on a bench on the seafront, looking out to sea.* CALLUM *looks through a pair of binoculars at the sea.*

They have two bottles next to them, one cider, one ale. GUSSIE *drinks the cider,* CALLUM, *the ale, intermittently.*

CALLUM. A vampire?

GUSSIE. Needed askin', man. She's probably one of they Goths that sucks the blood oo-ay hamsters.

CALLUM. I've changed my mind about you. You are doolally.

GUSSIE. No' crazy enough to fancy her.

CALLUM. Nor me.

GUSSIE. Saw the way you were flirtin'.

CALLUM. Wasnae flirtin'. She's no' my type.

GUSSIE. Beggars can't be choosers.

CALLUM. I am choosy.

GUSSIE (*sarcastic*). Of course ye are. There was me thinkin' your eighteen years of celibacy were cos you're a deadweight wi' birds.

CALLUM. Fuck off. Boat out there, by the way. Forty-five degrees.

GUSSIE. Dinnae worry, mate, she's probably no' worth it anyhow. Cockney. All jellied eels and cockles. In ten years she'll look like Pat Butcher.

CALLUM. You were oo-ay order wi' her.

Beat.

GUSSIE. Fuck it, I know, I get… I see red. I cannae be done wi' folks lookin' at us as if we're shite. I'm no' shite.

CALLUM. Yer no'.

GUSSIE. Just genetically light-fingered!

GUSSIE *takes* HARRIET*'s handbag out of his coat.*

CALLUM. No, Gussie! That hers?

GUSSIE. Finders keepers. She should be grateful I'm looking after this for her. The speed she ran off. (*Picking up the handbag and sifting through it.*) Why do birds carry so much crap around in these things?

GUSSIE *pulls out a packet of tissues, a tampon and a mascara wand. He opens the mascara –*

You know, she'll wantae reward me for my dashing behaviour.

You wouldnae mind, would ye, seein' as you're no' interested.

– and dabs CALLUM*'s cheek.*

CALLUM. Fuck off! Leave her stuff alone, man. She'll go mad when she finds us wi' this.

GUSSIE *pulls out her purse, opens it and reads out from the cards he takes out.*

GUSSIE. HSBC. Own bank account. Very fancy. Southwark College. Got brains. Lambeth Library. Ooh-hoo, could be as geeky as you.

CALLUM. Am no' geeky.

GUSSIE. No, yer no'. Ye've just got an intense interest in numbers and books. No' geeky at all.

Could show her all the diagrams and charts in yer wee book.

CALLUM. Numbers the only thing that's written in it wi' you pishin' about. Boat oot there. Forty-five degrees east.

GUSSIE. What else am I gonna do? Am no' gettin' a go o' them, am I?

CALLUM. It's gotta be done properly. If you want answers to questions you've got tae be methodical. It's like a science study. We have a goal: to find out if it was a dead woman, and this is our data collection.

GUSSIE. Jesus fuckin' Christ. Tell ye, I'm checking my birth certificate.

Giz a go o' them.

CALLUM. There's nothing to see the noo.

GUSSIE (*handling* HARRIET's *debit card*). Maybe I'll nip down the shops.

CALLUM *takes the binoculars away from his eyes.*

CALLUM. No!

GUSSIE. Ha ha, giz them then.

CALLUM. You gotta handle them properly.

CALLUM *reluctantly hands over the binoculars to* GUSSIE, *who immediately puts them to his eyes and looks around.* CALLUM *picks up the handbag and purse and carefully puts the cards back.*

GUSSIE. Ach, no action oot at sea. No' even a horizon.

Aye aye. Ninety degrees, what do I see? Now I ken why you were lookin' that way. Wonder what she's looking for?

CALLUM. Aye, I wonder!

GUSSIE. Thinking how much she loves me.

CALLUM. I thought you didnae like her.

GUSSIE. Maybe I do.

Cannae help but notice you've gone very quiet about getting out of here. What's happened to going to London and getting a flat and setting up a new life, eh?

CALLUM. Am enjoyin' doing this. Me and you. S'no' like we've done much fun together recent, is it?

CALLUM *takes the binoculars*.

GUSSIE. Funny how I don't quite believe you.

Pause. CALLUM *puts down the binoculars*.

CALLUM. Y'know something, Gussie, I wouldnae mind a bird now.

GUSSIE. You jokin'? Had no idea!

Get that in London. Some lassie tae tickle your todger.

CALLUM. No… Someone who'll know you (*Points to his solar plexus*.) here. And you can… their heartbeat and that. I would love to hear a bird's heart beat.

GUSSIE. Wi' yer face squashed between her baps.

CALLUM. Something special. There's nothin' special here.

GUSSIE. Cheery soul, you today, eh.

CALLUM. This is serious. Wee bitta joy. Life is no' a dress rehearsal.

GUSSIE (*disgusted by the cliché*). Oh, for fuck's sake!

Beat.

You know, she seems quite posh, her. All her stuff is top-quality. You gotta wonder what she's doing up here.

CALLUM. Maybe it's a wee holiday.

GUSSIE *takes one of* HARRIET*'s letters out of his back pocket.*

GUSSIE. No, look.

CALLUM. Fuck's sake! There anything of hers you havenae got?

GUSSIE. Just her undying love, pal, but it'll come!

GUSSIE *reads from the letters.*

Listen to this. 'My darling, come and see me', 'I really miss you', 'Dinnae worry about what your mother says.'

CALLUM *looks through the binoculars.*

CALLUM. Ssssh. Wait a minute! What's that? Look!

GUSSIE. Driftwood.

CALLUM (*pointing*). No, look!

GUSSIE. Jesus, man. Is that what I think it is?

CALLUM. Aye! See its head?

GUSSIE. Black eyes.

CALLUM. A seal?

GUSSIE. That's no' what we saw the other night.

CALLUM *passes* GUSSIE *the binoculars.*

CALLUM. Ye dinnae know that. (*Fetching the book.*) Never thought… This is big, bro. This is fuckin' big.

Any others?

GUSSIE. Lookin' this way. It's just bobbin' there, man.

CALLUM (*writing*). What else can ye see?

The colour, Gussie? Markings.

GUSSIE *puts the binoculars down, stands and looks out to sea. He waves.* CALLUM *tries to write but the pen has run out of ink.*

Don't scare it.

GUSSIE. It's starin' at us.

CALLUM. Aye.

GUSSIE. Straight at us. Same as the body the other night.

CALLUM. Pass me the other pen, man.

GUSSIE. I havenae got it.

CALLUM. I gae it you before.

GUSSIE. No, ye –

CALLUM. Go and get another, wee man. Quick. Quick.

GUSSIE. Ach.

> GUSSIE *exits*. CALLUM *looks around and sees* HARRIET *approaching. He sits on her handbag, covering it.*

HARRIET. Oi, what ya doin'?

CALLUM. Nothing.

HARRIET. Why you lookin' all sly then? I saw ya, pointin' those things at us.

CALLUM. Wasnae. Straight up.

HARRIET. You shouldn't spy on people.

Why were you lookin' at me? Gettin' creeped out.

CALLUM. No, no, making observations. We were looking for a dead bird and now we're looking at a seal. Want a look?

> HARRIET *looks at him as if he's weird.* CALLUM *is distracted and continues to look out to sea.*

Maybe might even see some o' ye mates.

HARRIET. Ain't no friend of mine down there.

CALLUM. You no' got any pals?

HARRIET. Course I have. I look like a loner to you or something?

CALLUM. Aye, you do. You look like you're lost, Harriet. Like you need help, eh?

HARRIET. I don't. I'm sorted and I don't need nothing. 'Cept my handbag.

CALLUM. You lost it?

HARRIET. Disappeared like magic, last night.

29

CALLUM. Wasnae us. We don't need to steal. We're loaded.

HARRIET. Look at the way you dressed. They ain't the clothes of a rich type. If I was loaded I ain't gonna be hangin' out in dirty shell suit.

CALLUM. This Adidas.

HARRIET. Adidas has three stripes.

CALLUM (*counting the stripes running down his tracksuit bottoms*). Aye, and one for luck.

HARRIET *moves to leave.*

CALLUM. Where you goin'?

HARRIET. I don't talk to bullshitters, mate. I'm only here cos I believed some lie.

CALLUM. What lie?

HARRIET. A lie that said I should come here. Made me leave my mates and sister. Now everything gone shit. You gonna give us me bag?

CALLUM. Havenae got it. Straight up.

HARRIET. My life's in it, man. I gotta use my phone.

CALLUM. I can find it.

HARRIET. Don't bullshit me.

CALLUM. I'll prove it, bring it round yer house.

HARRIET. No way.

CALLUM. I'll find it. Where d'ye reside currently?

HARRIET. You find my bag and you'll find my address in it.

Enter GUSSIE.

GUSSIE. All right, beautiful?

HARRIET. Was.

GUSSIE. What dae ye mean by that?

HARRIET. Nothing. I'm goin'.

GUSSIE. Wait up, hen. Offer of a double cheese is still on.

HARRIET. Laters, yeah.

Exit HARRIET.

GUSSIE. Face like a slapped arse, her. Dunno why I'm botherin'. What did she say about me?

CALLUM. When?

GUSSIE. Just now.

CALLUM. Didnae mention you. Talkin' about the weather.

GUSSIE. No' my teeth?

CALLUM. What about yer teeth?

GUSSIE. I've always had nice teeth.

CALLUM. No' a word. Liked my trousers, though.

GUSSIE. Them? Fuck's sake. She cannae fuckin' like you!

CALLUM. Like I say, wee man, she's no' my type. No' interested.

GUSSIE. We'll keep it like that.

Beat. CALLUM *takes the binoculars and looks out to sea.*

Scene Six

Later that day. CALLUM *is sitting outside* HARRIET's *dad's house. He has washed his hair and combed it back. He wears an old-fashioned shirt that has seen better days, his jeans and trainers. He holds a bunch of flowers (mainly dead stalks) that he has picked from the local park and carries* HARRIET's *handbag. He shivers. After checking his watch, he throws a stone at* HARRIET's *window.*

CALLUM. Hey!

(*Under his breath.*) Shite.

He throws another stone at her window. Pause. HARRIET *approaches from the side of the house.*

HARRIET. You gonna smash that winda.

CALLUM. Thought you were up there.

HARRIET. Shouldn't assume nothing, should ya.

CALLUM. What you doin' by the bins?

HARRIET. Waiting for you and my bag. You got it?

CALLUM. Oh aye.

HARRIET. Surprise, that.

CALLUM. Found it by the steps.

HARRIET. Lucky me. Didn't think you'd show up.

CALLUM. Aye, I said I would. Here I am.

HARRIET. Yeah. Here you are.

CALLUM. Aye.

HARRIET. So?

CALLUM. Um, well… I, er… you know, thought we could… er, go out first.

HARRIET. Where?

CALLUM. A walk.

HARRIET. I don't need nothin'.

CALLUM. To the pier or summat. Burger King. Paint the town red, eh.

CALLUM *holds out the flowers to* HARRIET. *Beat.*

HARRIET. They for me?

CALLUM. They're no' much.

HARRIET. No, they ain't.

I thought you was just comin' to give us me bag.

CALLUM. I am but I thought you might like tae…

HARRIET. What?

CALLUM. The cliff's amazing this time o' year. Beautiful looking across the mist on the Forth.

HARRIET. I got heels. Ain't walkin'.

CALLUM. It's our special place, me and my brother. It's nice.

HARRIET. If ya gonna top yaself.

CALLUM. You can look at things. I could gaze at the stars for hours up there.

HARRIET. Jesus, man, that is so cheesy.

CALLUM. Serious I can. My binoculars are variable focus.

HARRIET. Man, you gotta work on your lines.

I don't give a shit about the moon.

Just giz me bag, yeah.

CALLUM *gives her the handbag*.

Cheers.

CALLUM *stares at the pavement*.

See ya then.

Pause.

CALLUM. You no' goin' in?

HARRIET. Yeah, in a minute.

CALLUM. You no' freezin'?

HARRIET. Yeah, I know, it winter.

CALLUM. You want my shirt?

HARRIET. I'll be fine. Got me bags there. (*Points*.) You go on back to your little brother, man.

CALLUM. Aye, I will.

CALLUM *doesn't leave*.

HARRIET. What? Ain't got my keys, have I?

CALLUM. Knock on the door then.

HARRIET. Not in.

CALLUM. When they coming back?

HARRIET. Dunno. Look, I dunno. I been knocking.

CALLUM. For how long?

HARRIET. A while.

Beat.

CALLUM. Is it a friend?

HARRIET. No. No, it ain't.

It's my dad.

CALLUM. He knows yer coming?

HARRIET. Yeah, I told him. Got letter from him Friday. He were all excited. Said he was missing us bad. He was gonna meet us at the station. But he [didn't] …

Maybe he gone out. He does get forgetful sometimes.

CALLUM. How long you been waiting then?

HARRIET. Not long. Couple of days.

CALLUM. By the bins?

HARRIET. The beach yesterday. So I only really been waiting here a day. He coulda come back while I was, you know…

Pause.

CALLUM. So what if yer daddy doesnae come back?

HARRIET. You saying he's a liar?

CALLUM. But if. You might have noticed this is no' the sunniest and driest part of the world.

HARRIET. I'll kip round the side. Don't matter. Not like I can afford… hotel; I spent everything getting here, didn't I?

CALLUM. Aye, you know, I… at ours. We've got a spare room now.

HARRIET. No, I don't know you, man. And your brother scares me, y'know. All the vampire shit.

CALLUM. If you promise to no' suck his blood, he wouldnae mind. It's no' hot but it's no' wet either. It's got a mirror and dresser and somewhere to put yer clothes. S'all ready. It's no' been touched since…

Pause.

34

HARRIET. Sweet of ya, but I can't. Just in case.

CALLUM. If you change yer mind.

HARRIET. No.

CALLUM *takes the £100 out of his pocket.*

CALLUM. Look, this is a hundred. There's a B&B next to Woolies.

HARRIET (*shakes her head*). No.

CALLUM. C'mon. Yer no' safe out here.

HARRIET. My dad coming back.

CALLUM *holds out the money.*

CALLUM. Harriet?

HARRIET. Fuck off! Just fuck off! He coming back! How can you think he ain't coming back?!

Scene Seven

Next day. The cliff top. Below is the beach. CALLUM stares out to sea, drinking a can of Irn-Bru. There are fish-and-chip wrappers next to him. There is a notebook and pen by his feet. Beside him, GUSSIE is looking through the binoculars, pointed out to sea. He is sulking. There is a lengthy silence. GUSSIE picks up the book from CALLUM's feet, all the while scowling at him. He jots down some numbers in the book. CALLUM slurps noisily. He shakes the can for drops and screws up the fish-and-chip paper.

CALLUM. Record and a carry-oot. Like the old days, Gussie? Remember, man?

He looks for a reaction but gets none. He throws the ball of paper over the cliff.

Aye, ye dae so. Heaven.

Slight pause.

(*Re: the seal.*) Where is it?

GUSSIE *throws the book at CALLUM sulkily.*

35

(*Picks up the book and reads*.) Twenty-three?

Fifty-six, thirty-one, twenty-three. That's closer. She knows we're here. A fuckin' seal, man! Must trust us now.

Gussie? (*Annoyed*.) Oi. Oi! You gonna talk tae me?

GUSSIE. Made a racket comin' in last night. Wee bit late for you.

Gone somewhere special, was it?

CALLUM. What's it to you?

GUSSIE. Interested, that's all.

CALLUM. What's with the tone?

GUSSIE. Noticed ye washed yer hair. Wondered what that could mean.

CALLUM. That it was dirty?

GUSSIE. Brushed yer teeth. No' every day ye brush yer teeth. Did she like yer clean shirt?

CALLUM. Deh ken what you're talking about.

GUSSIE. Fuck off, ye dinnae! She's my bird, man! I saw her first!

CALLUM. Maybe I was out. Maybe I was just helpin' out a mate who needs a bit a help, like.

GUSSIE. Our money?

CALLUM. Maybe.

GUSSIE. How can Queen o' the Damned need it more than us? Is she stealin' everything she eats? We're no' a charity. We're the fuckin' Children in Need.

CALLUM. I know, Gussie. Am no' stupid.

GUSSIE. Ye finished school. Ye've got something between your ears. Am relying on you to, ye know, no' be the eejit one.

CALLUM. I'm just offering a wee bit of help.

GUSSIE. Nobody helps us.

CALLUM. Exactly! So why no' try and change things a bit?

GUSSIE. So it's out of the goodness of your heart?

CALLUM. Aye.

GUSSIE. No' tae get yer end away?

CALLUM. No!

GUSSIE. Aye, I believe that. (*He looks through the binoculars.*)
We're the two musketeers, Callum. One for one.

CALLUM. It's no' what you think it is. Straight up. I wasnae out
with Harriet last night. I'm no' gonna put anyone over ye.

GUSSIE. Nineteen.

CALLUM. I said I won't, Gussie.

GUSSIE. Nineteen.

CALLUM. You're my brother.

GUSSIE (*stressing*). Nineteen.

Beat.

CALLUM. Nineteen!

GUSSIE. She's right in.

CALLUM. This time tomorrow and she'll be on the beach.

GUSSIE. At this rate. Imagine that, a seal on the beach, standing
there on the beach.

CALLUM. Standing?

GUSSIE. Standing. Remember all they fuckin' stories? The fairy
stories.

CALLUM. Nae time for fairy stories.

GUSSIE. Why not? Wee bit o' a coincidence. Body in the water,
then next day it's turned intae a seal. Remember the stories,
Callum. As the tide comes in, the seals come in.

CALLUM. C'mon, buddy, we're no' five.

GUSSIE. They'll be wanting to come on land and shed their skin.
Turn back to what they were. They'll no' be seals any more.
They'll be –

CALLUM. That's enough, Gussie. Eh? That's enough.

GUSSIE. You'll no' be doubting when you see her.

CALLUM. Look again!

GUSSIE *looks through the binoculars.*

GUSSIE. Callum, she's gone! I cannae see her.

CALLUM *shoves* GUSSIE *out of the way and looks through the binoculars.*

She's cannae have gone, Callum!

CALLUM. Where was she, Gussie? She cannae hae disappeared.

GUSSIE. It's where it's pointed. Out there. I could see her head. She was bobbin' like a buoy.

CALLUM. Ah Jesus! She's nowhere. I cannae get her.

GUSSIE. Look harder!

CALLUM. Where?! It's pretty fuckin' dark, man. There's only moonlight.

GUSSIE. That way. (*Left.*) See her?

CALLUM. Nut.

CALLUM *looks through the binoculars and then down, bringing the view closer to the beach.*

GUSSIE. Shit! Where can she be?

CALLUM. Maybe she's diving. She's no' gonna be closer tonight. They don't come in too close. She'll be away on the rocks.

Jesus!

CALLUM *lays down on the cliff top and peers over the side, down to the beach.*

GUSSIE. What?

CALLUM (*pointing to the beach*). Look.

GUSSIE *falls on his front next to* CALLUM. *His face drops. Enter* HARRIET. *They do not see her. She stands and watches.*

(*Pointing.*) There. She's beautiful.

GUSSIE. Sittin' in the fuckin' surf.

CALLUM (*whispering*). She's really lookin' at us now, Gussie.

GUSSIE. What'll I do? Shout?

CALLUM. No. Let her get used tae us.

Beat.

GUSSIE. Cannae believe it.

Sorry I went off at ye, bro. (*Extending his hand for* CALLUM *to shake.*) Lost my head.

CALLUM (*shaking his hand*). No worries. Doesnae matter any more. Get the book, wee man.

GUSSIE *moves to retrieve his book. He sees* HARRIET. *They freeze when they see each other.* GUSSIE *looks from* HARRIET *to* CALLUM *to* HARRIET *and then* CALLUM *again. He shakes his head in disgust. He begins hastily packing up his things.*

It's no' what you're thinking, Gussie, c'mon.

GUSSIE. I cannae fuckin' believe it.

HARRIET. I didn't know you two was serious about bein' stargazers. Dark horses, ent ya? What you two up to then?

GUSSIE. He hasnae got any more cash for ye.

CALLUM. Gussie.

GUSSIE. 'I wouldnae put anyone over you, Gussie. You're my brother.'

HARRIET *wanders around their area.* GUSSIE *finishes packing up. He leaves the binoculars.*

HARRIET (*to* CALLUM). I wanted to say something. Last night.

GUSSIE. Nice, was it?

HARRIET. Yeah. So what?

GUSSIE. You noticed he cleaned his teeth? And washed his hair. No' even for our mammy's funeral did he wash his hair.

HARRIET. Your mum's dead?

CALLUM. That's oo-ay order, wee man.

GUSSIE. You'd know about oo-ay order.

HARRIET. You never said.

GUSSIE. Aye, she's dead. She's dead and she's left us.

Pause.

HARRIET (*seeing the book*). Why you writin' numbers down?

GUSSIE (*taking the book from her*). Dinnae touch that. It's ours. (*Shouts.*) Callum!

CALLUM. You'll scare it, shouting.

GUSSIE *looks panicked and goes back to the cliff top.*

GUSSIE. She's gone! Fuck's sake! Callum, she's gone! (*To* HARRIET.) Look what you've fuckin' done. You've ruined it!

CALLUM *walks to the cliff.*

Are you comin'?

CALLUM. Giz a minute.

GUSSIE. I'm your brother, Callum. I'm the only fuckin' one you've got. No' fuckin' her. I'm your blood, man. What'd Mammy say if she could see – ?

CALLUM. Not Mammy, Gussie!

GUSSIE. She'd be cut to the quick by you. The only family left living and look what yer doin'. Me and you!

GUSSIE *doesn't take his eyes off* CALLUM. *He shakes his head.*

CALLUM. Gussie?!

GUSSIE *looks distraught. He picks up the binoculars and exits.* CALLUM *looks over his shoulder to where* GUSSIE *has run off. Silence.*

HARRIET. At least he never called us a vampire this time.

CALLUM. What you doin' here?

HARRIET. I was thinkin' about you today, man. I was harsh on you last night.

HARRIET *takes the money out of her handbag and holds it out to* CALLUM.

I thought you should have this back.

CALLUM. Did yer daddy come back?

HARRIET. No, but maybe tonight, eh.

Pause.

I'm really sorry about your mum. I didn't know.

CALLUM. Don't worry. I'm trying to no' think about it. You gotta move on, leave the past behind.

HARRIET. He not moving on?

CALLUM. No. Keeps seein' her in his dreams. Talking to him. Saying she's no' happy and she's missing him and she wants to come back.

HARRIET. You worry about him, don't ya?

CALLUM. Truth, aye I do. It's like he's wired, all the time.

I'm trying to stop him thinking about it. I got this plan, see. My pal's got a job down your way. We're goin' tae kip on his floor. I'm going intae catering and Gussie, he'll dae kitchen portering.

HARRIET. You got it all planned, ent ya?

CALLUM. Aye, he needs to be told what to do.

CALLUM *sits on the cliff edge.*

HARRIET. Do you have to go?

CALLUM. Aye.

HARRIET. It's just… you know… Be nice if you didn't.

HARRIET *approaches gingerly. She sits down next to him.*

CALLUM. There's nothing to stop you coming down too.

HARRIET. No, there is, man.

CALLUM. What is it?

HARRIET. I can't / say.

CALLUM. Go / on.

HARRIET. I CAN'T! All right. You don't wanna know. If you wanna keep likin' me, don't ask.

Pause. HARRIET *gazes over the cliff edge.*

CALLUM. You all right?

HARRIET. Long way down, innit.

CALLUM. Scared?

HARRIET. It's so dark. If you fell, no one would know you was down there. You not worried you might fall?

CALLUM. Honest. No. Don't think anyone would mind anyway.

HARRIET. I'm worried you'll fall.

CALLUM. You'd catch me?

HARRIET. You'd do the same for me. That's the sorta person you are.

CALLUM. What if ye couldn't and I hit the bottom?

HARRIET. I'd look over. Then give it ten minutes of you screaming so I'd know comin' down was worth my while. Then if you was still howlin', I'd make sure I was wearing the right shoes, think about makin' my way down careful. Then I'd find you all cut up and bleedin'. Have a fag. Then I'd take you in my arms, keep you warm, and wrap you up in cotton wool.

They both think about kissing but don't. Awkward pause.
CALLUM *stands and begins dismantling the binoculars.*

CALLUM. It's cold here, no. We better go and find yer daddy.

HARRIET. Ain't you gonna tell me what you been lookin' at?

CALLUM. Will you tell me why you've run away from home?

HARRIET. C'mon, I bet it wicked. Is it treasure? Or shipwreck?

CALLUM. Harriet, will ye?

HARRIET. I'll give you a lolly. Wagon Wheel. Please.

I will tell ya but I wanna hear you first.

CALLUM. Ye cannae laugh.

HARRIET. Course not, man. I gotta poker face.

CALLUM. Serious. You gotta promise.

HARRIET. I do. (*She crosses her heart.*)

CALLUM *walks to the edge of the cliff. Beat.*

What's down there, man?

CALLUM. Our mammy.

Don't laugh. Few days ago. We saw our mammy in the water.
We saw her in the water. Just out, there, fifty metres.

'It's a log,' I said, 'a sea buoy.'

But there's legs, and I saw arms. I saw her pink arms. I shut my
eyes, cos it couldn't be. She's no' there, I telt myself. I looked
again and no mistake. Bobbing. The hair, fanning out. We just
stared, no' movin'.

But then. Gussie's in the freezing water up to his knees, about to
swim. I'm sayin', 'No, Gussie, stop.' But he's no' hearin'.

What could I do? I stood there. And he's stood there. She's
floating. We're shivering.

I'm willing her – float in. Come in.

'Callum?' he says. 'Think it's Mammy?' And I shake my head.
'No. Let her be. She'll come if she wants to.'

Pause.

HARRIET. And what?

CALLUM. Out she goes, floats. Us two frozen to where we're
standing.

He's sayin' she's one of them.

CALLUM *walks back.*

HARRIET. One of what, man?

CALLUM. Fairy stories. This is stupid. Nothing but stories we got
told as kids, you know.

HARRIET. Like what?

CALLUM. You heard of the selkie folk? They're spirits, like
fairies, aye, but they take the form of seals living in the sea.
They'll no' bother ye unless you do something tae offend them.
If you do… they come for ye. Take ye under the water, roll ye
round at the bottom of the sea and turn you into one of them.

Our mammy used to tell us they stories. And say the selkies would come and get us, you know if… and there was one story about folks if they died young or at the wrong time, the selkies would come and take 'em and have them as their own. And they live with them until they wanted to come home and finish their life. When they were ready, they'd come into shore and onto the beach and turn back into the person they were. And everyone would be happy and everything would be the same as it was.

Scene Eight

Later that day. Shirts, jeans, T-shirts, socks are raining down from the sky. CALLUM is outside their house. The front door is locked. There is a window next to the wall. CALLUM is soaking wet and angry. He beats off the clothes. GUSSIE throws more clothes from the window at him. GUSSIE throws a packet of Kellogg's Frosties from the window at CALLUM.

CALLUM. No' ma Frosties, man!

GUSSIE leans out of the window. He has a black eye.

GUSSIE. You're no' comin' in!

Ye can fuck off tae ye fancy bit, Callum, why don't ye.

CALLUM begins picking up his clothes.

CALLUM. Let us in, ye wee prick.

It's pishin' it down. Am gonna drown out here.

GUSSIE puts two fingers up at the window.

Wee fucker.

Open this fuckin' door.

GUSSIE. I've got nothing to say to you.

That seal's our mammy. She's come to the beach, Callum, you've seen her and ye dinnae give a fuck.

CALLUM. I do, man.

GUSSIE leans out of the window further.

GUSSIE. No, you don't. You've lost sight. Your eye's off the ball. You're too busy fuckin' about with Dracula. This is our fuckin' mammy, man.

CALLUM. I'm doin' this with ye, Gussie.

GUSSIE. Don't fuck wi' me, Callum. Yer tryin' to get your end away. Just a fuckin' game tae ye.

CALLUM. Would I have been there on they cliffs if this was a game? I wanna find oot. This thing.

GUSSIE. She's no' a thing. Our mammy's no' a thing.

CALLUM. You know what I mean.

GUSSIE. That's just fuckin' it. It's no' real tae you, is it?

You know what you saw.

CALLUM. Aye, I know what I think I saw.

GUSSIE. Floatin' in front of our eyes. Out there. I could see her face and her fingers. I coulda run and got her.

CALLUM. Let us in, Gussie.

GUSSIE. No. No' until you admit it.

CALLUM. Admit what?

GUSSIE. That what we saw was real. It was oor mammy. She's come to find us.

Beat.

CALLUM. But how can it be real?

If I said it to ye now, ye'd laugh in my face.

The selkies, wee man, they're just a fairy tale. A folk livin' under the sea as seals. C'mon, please.

GUSSIE. You can laugh it up.

CALLUM. I'm no' / sayin' that.

GUSSIE. Just cos you don't know doesn't mean it doesnae exist.

You'd be one of they folks who said the world was flat.

CALLUM. Let us in, eh.

GUSSIE. I wanna hear you say this no' just a story –

CALLUM. Of course it's a story. That's what stories are, made up. You got more chance o' seein' Santa.

GUSSIE. You laughin' at me?

CALLUM. She'll no' be on the beach. They're loads o' other reasons, other theories. Ye cannae believe the first thing –

GUSSIE. Am waitin' on tha beach till she comes. You're comin' wi' us.

CALLUM. And what if she doesnae. If it's just a seal?

GUSSIE. We'll cross that bridge –

CALLUM. Then get oo-ay here. Next week, imagine yersel' doon by the Thames, eh. We'll go on the Eye, wi' ice creams and Cokes. And the Tower of London and Crown Jewels and get a place, a flat, the two o' us. Parties and mates and… you know, mates. Agreed? Gussie?

Beat.

S'all right. I know why you wanna see her.

GUSSIE. Tell us then, genius.

GUSSIE *steps out of the window and towards* CALLUM.

CALLUM. Cos you werenae there for her, were yer? When I was down the hospice, wiping the spit off her chin and fixin' her pilly, you were off out.

Even till the day she died, man. Always up tae shite.

GUSSIE. She knew I was –

I brought her flowers from the garage.

I gave cash tae the Cancer Research shop, man.

You, Callum, you werenae model.

CALLUM. No, I fuckin' wasnae. But I wasnae you.

GUSSIE. I was good. I was a good son. (*Sits on the pavement in a ball.*) The trouble… I never meant tae… (*He buries his head in his knees and cries.*)

Beat. CALLUM *sits next to* GUSSIE.

CALLUM. What's that on yer face?

GUSSIE. Nothin'.

CALLUM *inspects the bruise,* GUSSIE *winces.*

Fell. Stairs.

CALLUM. How many times? Who did this? How many of them were there?

CALLUM *takes his sock off and soaks it in the cold water on the steps.*

GUSSIE. I couldnae see. Jumped out on us by Bentleys. Eight or nine or...

CALLUM. You say anythin' to 'em?

GUSSIE. Of course no'.

One o' them said somethin' about neds. Posh cunt, he was. Banker.

Maybe I lamped him first...

CALLUM *tries to put it on* GUSSIE*'s brow.*

Aw, fuck off! That's stinkin'! Your stinkin' feet.

CALLUM. They were clean last week.

He puts it to GUSSIE*'s brow.*

GUSSIE. [It's] Cold.

CALLUM. Hold it there.

Beat.

Gussie, you're my brother. Everything I do is for you. You're the only fuckin' one in my life.

GUSSIE. No' her.

CALLUM. You say the word and I'm here. Whatever I'm doin' I will drop for you. You know that. I know you do.

GUSSIE. It's no' feelin' like it.

CALLUM. You're my brother, man. I fuckin' love ye. You stupid cunt, I love you.

GUSSIE *hangs his head.*

So, are we pals again?

GUSSIE. You'll no' see her again then?

CALLUM. Dinnae ask me that.

GUSSIE. That's no' what ye just said.

CALLUM. I said I'd be here for ye. I cannae…

GUSSIE. No' what you said!

GUSSIE *storms inside the house.*

I'll throw ye oot a pilly.

CALLUM. She fuckin' likes me, man. I've met a bird that fuckin' likes me!

Scene Nine

3 a.m. CALLUM *is asleep and snoring outside* HARRIET's *dad's house. Enter* HARRIET *through the front door. She is in her pyjamas and trainers, not tied. She crouches down next to* CALLUM *and shakes him gently.*

HARRIET. Hey.

CALLUM *comes to, sleepily.*

There a fine line between likin' and stalkin', y'know.

CALLUM. How did you know / I was – ?

HARRIET. Heard you. Sounded like someone strangling a pig. (*She snores.*) I was dreaming someone drilling up the road.

You shouldn't be sleeping in the rain.

CALLUM (*pointing to the plastic bags*). Wee bastard's no' lettin' me in. Gone all green-eyed monster about me and… Y'know.

HARRIET. You shoulda knocked.

CALLUM. Ye're in?

HARRIET. Yeah, man. I let myself in the back. With a key made out of a brick.

CALLUM. Did ye – ?

(*Realising*.) That's illegal, you know.

HARRIET (*sarcastic*). Really?

CALLUM. Polis could have you up breakin' and enterin'.

HARRIET. Don't care, man. I weren't gettin' in any other way. I been in every pub and shop and club and everythin'. Nothing. No one knows him, seen him. Makin' me think summink happened to him.

CALLUM. Serious?

HARRIET. Gotta be.

Pause.

CALLUM. I'll get that windae fixed. Get it swept up. Don't wanna step on the glass.

HARRIET. Man, you is classic! You so serious.

CALLUM. I'm no' being serious.

HARRIET. You said that even seriouser than before!

CALLUM. Seriouser's no' a proper word, ye know.

HARRIET *laughs*.

HARRIET. You classic. Sit back down here.

CALLUM *fidgets*.

What?

CALLUM. He's no' gonna be happy with / finding –

HARRIET. The window? Fuck him, man! I ain't happy with him! That ain't all he should be thinking when he crawl back! Am gonna be like a fury when I see him! Am gonna beat him and the bitch he live with.

I got my exams next month, man. I given up everything.

CALLUM. You should go in.

HARRIET. Nah, it ain't that bad out here. I'm a Taurus, yeah. That means I'm properly pigheaded.

CALLUM roots around in his bag. He pulls out a jumper.

Ain't pregnant. You don't have to try all that 'gentleman' shit.

CALLUM. Serious. Winnie the Pooh's only gonna keep you warm for so long.

She takes the jumper cautiously.

HARRIET. What make's this?

CALLUM. It's from the seventies. My dad's. The only thing he left when he ran out on us.

She puts on the jumper.

HARRIET. Ain't Diesel but it all right.

CALLUM. Warmer?

HARRIET nods.

HARRIET. You can do that 'yawn' thing now if you like, gentleman. You know, that –

She stretches her arm over and around his shoulders in a 'yawn' stretch. She then withdraws her arm.

CALLUM. I dunno.

HARRIET. Go on.

CALLUM. Cheesy! (*Points right.*) Look, a zombie.

As HARRIET looks to the right, distracted, he 'yawns' in an awkward way and puts his arm around her shoulder.

HARRIET. Ah, good man! Ha, you is good. That was proper sly.

She wriggles out of his grasp and 'yawns' and puts her arm around his shoulders.

CALLUM. Kinda freezin' here, eh.

HARRIET. You don't smell like I thought you would. Expectin' Oxfam shops.

CALLUM. Cheers. A charmer, you.

HARRIET. You should get used to insults. Everyone gonna insult you if you different from them. Makes them feel normal.

CALLUM. Gussie says I'm anal. Says I spend all day ironing pants and picking up litter.

HARRIET. You ain't then?

CALLUM. No. I can be wacky.

HARRIET. In a real way or in a 'I wear *Simpsons* socks' kind of way?

CALLUM. I can be a laugh.

HARRIET. Your bed, always made and pj's under ya pillow.

CALLUM. No!

HARRIET. Honest? All your CDs alphabetical.

CALLUM. I'm no' Rainman.

HARRIET. But it a yes, right?

CALLUM. Next question.

HARRIET. Bet ya always have matching socks.

CALLUM. No! Look!

He shows HARRIET *his socks.*

HARRIET. Impressive.

CALLUM. My turn. On you.

HARRIET. I ain't anal.

CALLUM. No, for you it's different. You think you're a wee bit different from other folk, right. Aye, wi' yer black and that. Bet I can find three things about you that's so normal.

HARRIET. Try your luck, Jocko.

CALLUM. First up: You love it when people notice your hair's been cut. Aye?

Second: You'll believe anything if it's a compliment.

HARRIET. Shit, man.

CALLUM. Third: You've had a daydream about winning the lottery and you've worked out how much exactly you'd give all yer family and friends and exactly what you'd buy with it.

HARRIET. I don't care if I never won the lottery. Money ain't all that to me.

CALLUM. Only folk wi' money say that.

HARRIET. Very serious point.

You don't have to be serious all the time, you know. If things been shit up to now don't mean they have to stay that way. You gotta do what makes ya happy. Giz your arm. Roll up the sleeve.

She takes his arm in her hands and blows a raspberry on his arm.

That what I think about you bein' serious.

CALLUM (*wiping his arm*). The slobber!

HARRIET. You want another?

CALLUM. No! You're like a labrador!

He laughs. Beat. She pulls CALLUM*'s arm around her. Pause. They kiss. This time it is long and passionate.* CALLUM *puts his arm around* HARRIET. *They look out across the street.*

HARRIET. We is looking on the bright side. If you don't I'll wedgie you so bad you'll choke on your own pants.

CALLUM. Deal.

HARRIET. Where's Gussie now?

CALLUM. Home. He on tha beach the morn.

HARRIET. We gonna make it up with him. You gonna be his best brother again, right. Be mates.

She stands and takes his hand. She pulls him up. She leads him into the house.

C'mon. It's all right.

CALLUM. Yer daddy.

HARRIET. Keep me company.

Scene Ten

5 a.m. Half-light. HARRIET's *dad's stepdaughter's bedroom. The room has just a bed with 1980s-fashion sheets and a duvet. Her open suitcase is on the floor.* CALLUM *sits on the edge of the bed with his jeans in his hands, about to put them on.* HARRIET *is asleep.* CALLUM *reads from his open notebook. He looks anxious.* HARRIET *wakes up.*

HARRIET. Don't ya sleep?

CALLUM. I couldnae...

HARRIET. What ya doin'?

    CALLUM *begins to put on his trousers.*

CALLUM. 5 a.m., eh. Better go.

HARRIET. No, man, you gotta stay.

    What?

CALLUM. Bit weird, no. In a kid's room.

HARRIET. You think it woulda been less weird in my dad's bed?

CALLUM. It's just that Care Bear starin' at me. Spooking me out.

HARRIET. You can chuck it if ya want. It's Morag's, her daughter's.

CALLUM. Got lots o' nice things.

HARRIET. But not a real dad.

CALLUM. Looks like they left in a hurry.

HARRIET. All their stuff's gone, I've looked. Everything. Like they never existed.

    I been leaving messages, texting, going round the streets looking through people's windows, I thought, you know, maybe. I had faith, like I had faith he would call us, text us, something. But... you know.

CALLUM. S'all right. That's yer daddy lying. He's no different from anyone else. How do you know for sure anything's true? Wi' everything ye get told, I think about... I mean... I think, would I dream it up if no one had telt me.

HARRIET. Like what?

CALLUM. Aye, like, if the world began again tomorrow wi' everyone in it, and no one telt us God existed, why would you even think He did?

If we hadnae been telt of selkies, Gussie would never... you know. I cannae work out what we saw.

HARRIET. Maybe you was tricked by your eyes, yeah. I done that, when I real tired and wake up and see me bundle of clothes as, ya know, a clown or summink.

It sleepy logic. You was probably half-sleepin'.

CALLUM. But both of us?

HARRIET. Then maybe it was real. You can't know nuffin' for sure, can ya.

Pause.

Nice undies by the way. They Superman?

Giz a proper look.

CALLUM *stands and shows her his pants.*

Wish we'd had the light on now. Coulda clocked them. If I'd known you was wearing them the other night, I would've have had 'em off quicker.

CALLUM *sits on the edge of the bed self-consciously.*

Really, they sexy.

CALLUM. I've got Batman too. They're my lucky ones, though. These just... / you know.

HARRIET (*teasing*). They can be your lucky ones now.

CALLUM *begins putting on his trousers.*

Don't put them on yet.

CALLUM. Cold in here.

HARRIET. I wanna see ya. Sit here.

CALLUM *sits on the bed. He pulls his knees up self-consciously.*

Chill, yeah.

You kinda pale, ain't ya?

CALLUM. No' much sun in Fife. Apart from one day in August when the sky runs outta rain.

Pause.

Can I put the light on?

HARRIET. No. People will know we're here. I like this being just me and you. (*Exposing her chest.*) You think I got nice tits?

CALLUM (*embarrassed*). Aye, I dunno.

HARRIET. Look at me.

You think?

CALLUM (*uncomfortable*). They're lovely.

HARRIET. This one's bigger than that.

CALLUM. Didnae notice.

HARRIET. Just look at us. Stay there.

Slight pause.

Just look at each other. I wanna see ya as ya are. Look at me.

Slight pause.

Just look at me.

You got nice shoulders.

She runs her hands over his shoulders and chest.

It's all right, man. You like a coiled spring, ent ya?

Your hands.

She takes his hand and presses her palm against his and moves it together.

I want you to see me as I am, Callum. This the real me. I won't never tell you no lies. You promise the same for me?

CALLUM. Aye, I do.

They kiss. She hugs him hard.

HARRIET. I could hold ya like this for ever.

CALLUM. Can feel yer heart beat.

She laughs. She makes the sound of a heartbeat.

HARRIET. Drum 'n' bass, innit.

You won't lie to me, will ya?

CALLUM. Am no' good at it. Always go beetroot. Go ahead, ask me...

Pause. She thinks.

HARRIET. That the first time you done that last night?

CALLUM. No! Why?

HARRIET. No reason, man. Seemed a bit shy.

CALLUM. Was it yours?

HARRIET. Since I been up here.

CALLUM. Oh.

HARRIET. Bit like a Duracell Bunny, weren't ya?

CALLUM. Sorry.

HARRIET. It were nice, man.

CALLUM. Nice?

HARRIET. Yeah. I didn't mean that as –

It were real... like you, I dunno, it made me feel all warm inside. It was like it meant something special.

CALLUM. I think you're amazing, Harriet. The best thing in my life.

(*Confident.*) Would ye say it was one of the best?

HARRIET. One of.

CALLUM. The best?

HARRIET. Like Superman. You can write that in your book.

CALLUM *smiles and puts on his jeans.*

CALLUM. You've got a message. Your phone.

HARRIET *picks up the phone.*

HARRIET. Fuck.

HARRIET *reads the message.*

Must have a new phone.

HARRIET *uses the number to call. After a long ring, she connects.*

Dad? Oh, Carol. I want me dad. (*Listens to the reply.*) I know the time.

(*To* CALLUM.) She came in a package with the red motorbike, leather jacket and earring.

(*On the phone, excited.*) Dad, it's Harriet. Yeah, I know… ain't that early. But I never knew you had a new number. I been waiting outside your house for three days but I didn't know… (*Reply.*) I know but I didn't know. When did you move? (*Hushed reply.*) When? (*Reply.*) You never told us. (*Reply.*) I know but… (*Reply.*) Friday. (*Reply.*) Train. I been living out – I been waiting. (*Reply.*) Yeah, outside. I did call ya. About ten times but you never – left messages. (*Reply.*) Oh. (*Long reply.*) Busy. (*Short reply.*) Yeah, Mum's still down London. She's fine… (*Reply.*) I'll call her. (*Reply.*) Yeah, I will call her. So where are you now then? (*Pause.*) Dad, where are now? Dad? You still there? (*Pause.*) Dad, has she said something? (*Slight pause.*) I can hear… I can hear you breathing. Dad, where are you… ? Dad… (*Pause.*)

HARRIET *ends the call. She takes the letters out of the suitcase and sits. She begins to cry quietly.* CALLUM *sits next to her and tries to put his arm around her. She shakes her head and refuses his arm. She rips the letters up, becoming increasingly upset. She wipes her eyes.*

We gotta find your brother.

Scene Eleven

5.30 a.m. The beach. GUSSIE *walks along the surf, picking up flotsam (milk cartons, bits of driftwood and plastic) and putting them in piles. He wears his mother's scarf around his neck. Enter* HARRIET. *She watches him before approaching. The binoculars lie on top of the sand.*

HARRIET. This my favourite time; the morning when no one's around. Feels like the world's yours, don't it?

GUSSIE. Wouldn't know.

HARRIET. It's like watchin' a flower open up.

HARRIET picks up a bit of flotsam and adds it to the pile. She takes out the notebook.

GUSSIE. My brother no' with ye?

HARRIET. Gettin' food in the shop, yeah. He said give ya this.

HARRIET gives GUSSIE the notebook. He takes it.

You can say thanks.

She stoops over the pile and picks up a milk carton.

I know why you here, what you waiting for.

GUSSIE. No' for anything.

HARRIET. He told us about, you know… About your mum and stuff.

GUSSIE. He's lyin'. He's always lyin'.

Telt us Mammy was in hospital for a rest. For a week. Musta thought I was stupid.

HARRIET. He said you got numbers and you worked it out in ya book. That clever, innit.

GUSSIE. He did that. Ken thae people that cannae add up and folks say, 'They're good wi' their hands.' That's me. Except am no' great wi' ma hands.

HARRIET picks up the binoculars. She uses them to gaze out to sea.

You here tae take the pish then?

HARRIET. Course I ain't, man.

GUSSIE. Can if you want, I don't care. If I were you I would.

Just a bit of a laugh, though, this. It's no' as if we believe all the selkie crap. I mean, that's two steps away from bein' a looney tune.

HARRIET. It ain't a laugh, is it? You seen her yet? The seal?

You think she's comin'? You can tell me, man. It's all right.

GUSSIE. You? You're having a laugh.

HARRIET. You can trust me, mate.

GUSSIE. I'm no' that stupid. Everyone you trust lets you down.

HARRIET. I ain't like that. And your brother neither.

GUSSIE. Aye, right.

HARRIET. He a person too, yeah. He don't exist for you only.

Beat.

GUSSIE. Know what I wonder about ye? If I came from London, I wouldnae spend five minutes in this toon. We havnae even got a horizon.

HARRIET. Maybe I ain't stayin' that long. Things have changed.

GUSSIE. The fat man's charms no' worked on ye?

HARRIET. You got a nugget in him. He love ya more than himself.

Don't look at me like that, yeah. I never said I'd stay around for ever.

GUSSIE. I thought you said you were trustworthy?

HARRIET. I am. He knows… What am I supposed to do? I got nowhere to stay, no family.

GUSSIE. Welcome to oor world.

Pause.

Ye know, I was the one who liked you first. Saw you from the cliff. I thought you were a fuckin' beauty. It's supposed to be me and you.

HARRIET. You was so rude, man. I thought ya was such a dickhead.

Things don't always work out like you want. You know, you got get on with it and make best of –

GUSSIE. I cannae help it, man. Lose control of my trap.

HARRIET. Yeah, and it ain't even like I look like a vampire.

GUSSIE *is silent. He smiles.* HARRIET *realises he still thinks she does.*

(*Laughing.*) You cheeky bastard! I should stick these (*Re: binoculars.*) up your arse.

GUSSIE *takes his notebook out of his pocket. He opens it and reads the numbers.*

GUSSIE. She'll come in down there. Shouldn't be long.

HARRIET. What if she just a seal?

GUSSIE. Bet Callum fed ye that.

HARRIET. But what if, though?

GUSSIE. There's no ifs. It's got to be.

I'm no' leaving till I see her.

HARRIET *approaches and sits next to him.*

HARRIET. I know where you're comin' from. I get what you're thinkin'.

GUSSIE. Ye dinnae. Ye cannae.

HARRIET. I know you thinkin', 'Maybe this a bit mad, but maybe. Maybe she gonna just come.' And you know in your heart she ain't. But there a chance cos you ain't be proved wrong yet.

People believe in other things madder. They gonna win the lottery someday, but they never. Believe their love gonna last for ever, believe God see 'em through life.

Slight pause.

GUSSIE. You ever thought you were mental?

HARRIET. Once. I left my iPod on in my bag. Woke up hearin' these voices.

GUSSIE. I've heard voices in my dreams. Whispering. A little high voice. Like a wee girl. Talkin' to me. And last night. I was dreaming it was coming from the sink. Calling out.

HARRIET. How long you been hearing them?

GUSSIE. Dunno. While. I dream real funny, y'know. Like, every night they're weirder than the last. Mammy's there, always there. She said what I think is right.

HARRIET. [Does] Callum [know]?

GUSSIE *shakes his head. He picks up the binoculars and walks to the surf. He looks out to sea.* HARRIET *approaches.*

It ain't easy losing your mum, mate.

GUSSIE. You don't know what it's like. It's like a pain.

Twisting my guts. Every day the twist gets tighter.

Am no' crazy. It used to be me scrapin' Callum off the floor.

GUSSIE *wells up. He puts his hand over his eyes to cover them.* HARRIET *rubs his back.*

If this was last year, everything would be all right.

Bet you really do think I'm a loser now.

HARRIET. If you was that much of a loser before, (*Indicates with her thumb and forefinger.*) then now ya this. (*Indicates less with her fingers.*)

GUSSIE. Cheers.

HARRIET. S'all right. You bit of big girl for sobbin' but I'll forgive ya.

GUSSIE. What about me head? How much.

HARRIET *picks up two pebbles and puts them about a metre apart. Enter* CALLUM *carrying a bag of cans and food.* GUSSIE *and* HARRIET *do not see him.*

HARRIET. There's normal, (*Points.*) and there's loopy. (*Points.*) I'd say you was about… there. (*Just left of centre.*)

GUSSIE. No' David Icke yet then.

See, if that (*Points*.) was mingin' and that was beautiful, (*Points*.) that (*Beautiful*.) would be you.

GUSSIE *leans over and kisses* HARRIET. CALLUM *stops walking. He stares.* HARRIET *is shocked and doesn't react. He kisses her again.*

CALLUM *drops the bag. The noise makes* GUSSIE *and* HARRIET *jump. The three stare at each other in shock. Exit* CALLUM.

GUSSIE *and* HARRIET *stare at each other.* GUSSIE *leans in to kiss her again. She jerks her head back and shakes her head 'no'. She stands. Exit* HARRIET.

Scene Twelve

11 p.m. The beach. GUSSIE *sits alone. He looks disconsolately at his feet. He looks at his watch. He looks half-heartedly through the binoculars. He packs up his things. He holds his mother's scarf to his nose, stands and begins to walk away. He takes one last look over his shoulder. As he does, he notices a* WOMAN. *She is naked, deathly pale and has bruises on her body. Her hair is long and lank, tangled by the sea. Her eyes are all black like a seal's. She stands looking into the middle distance and then shuffles forward. And stops. She crouches down and inspects the sand.*

GUSSIE *is terrified. He shakes. She notices him and stares at him without breaking her gaze. Slowly he approaches her. He tentatively kneels in front of her. They stare at each other. He takes her hand and puts it to his hair on the side of his head. He moves her hand to his cheek. He holds it there. He removes his hand. The* WOMAN *keeps her hand on his cheek before moving it to his chin. Her hand then moves to his throat, tenderly for a moment, and then she begins to grip.* GUSSIE's *eyes widen.*

GUSSIE. No. No, Mammy.

Her hand grips tighter and tighter. He struggles trying to release the grip. It is too tight. The grip gets tighter and tighter. GUSSIE *blacks out.*

Scene Thirteen

The seafront. HARRIET is running to the train station, carrying her suitcase that has clothes spilling out of it. CALLUM runs behind her, and has been running behind her for a while.

CALLUM. Harriet, c'mon, you gotta wait up.

HARRIET. No, I gotta go. There's a train in five minutes.

CALLUM. Please, Harriet.

HARRIET. Ain't you listening to me? I don't wanna speak to / ya.

CALLUM. But –

HARRIET. You're like a dog, man, following me.

CALLUM. You know why, don't ya?

HARRIET. Yeah. You wanna have a fuckin' go. Slag me off, tell me I'm a bitch and you wish you'd never met us and you think you're better and I fuck off if I wanna cos you'll do so much better.

CALLUM. No!

HARRIET. Don't lie, man. You said you'd never lie.

You saw what happened. What it looked like.

CALLUM. Aye.

HARRIET. I weren't getting mouth to mouth.

CALLUM. I know.

HARRIET. Then why you still talking to us? Ain't you got no dignity? I ain't gonna sit outside someone's house all night if they cheated on me. Cos that's it, that's what you saw. Me, a cheat. I'm a worthless little bitch. Say it. That you see me and I'm scum. That's what I am. I know what you thinking. I know the way you think. I know you, Callum. I seen inside you –

CALLUM. Then you don't. You don't know me.

HARRIET. I do. You saw what happened.

CALLUM. Aye!

63

HARRIET. Then say something!

C'mon, say something.

HARRIET hits him.

CALLUM. Ow!

HARRIET. Hit us back then, eh.

CALLUM. No.

HARRIET. Tell us I'm a bitch. You know you wanna. C'mon, I know you wanna.

CALLUM. I don't. Please, / Harriet.

HARRIET. No.

She hits him. She tries to again and he puts his arms up.

CALLUM. Stop. Know what I saw? I saw my wee bastard brother plant one on you. You.

HARRIET. Yeah, me –

CALLUM. The shining light, fuckin', the best thing that's happened to me in my life. The one, I dunno… The best fuckin'… I dunno how to say it… you –

HARRIET. But…

CALLUM. But what?

HARRIET. I said I would never, I'd never lie to ya. Said I'd never do nothing untrue to ya. But there, I lost my head for a minute. I let it, I mean, I let him. I liked being told I was beautiful. I know it were bullshit but I fell for it, didn't I? I fuckin' fall for it, don't I?

CALLUM. Ye are, though. You're / so…

HARRIET. Nah, man, not here. (*Points to her heart.*) Am full of lies and stories just like everyone else.

CALLUM. Maybe. That makes you real, like everybody else. If what you see is what you get, then you'd be fuckin' boring. I don't want black and white.

Beat.

HARRIET. I wish I... I'm fuckin' sorry, man.

She takes her bags and moves off.

CALLUM. Don't run away.

HARRIET. Why not? It's what I do, innit. It what you doin' soon. I tell ya, it the answer cos then you never have to face up to nothing. Go down London, you think he ain't gonna miss his mum?

CALLUM. S'a new start.

HARRIET. It ain't, man. You can't run away from yourself. Take it from me.

CALLUM. So what you going back to face up tae?

HARRIET. Told ya, I can't tell ya. You'll hate me.

CALLUM. I'll no'. But how can I be open and honest wi' you if you're no' gontae be with me?

What happened to ye?

Long pause.

I'll see you then, eh.

HARRIET. No, wait up.

It were my mum.

CALLUM. Yer mammy?

HARRIET. I didn't mean but... She found the letters my dad sent. Said I were siding with him. She lost it, right. Was chucking stuff, saying I were sly, worthless, just like him. And a cup she chucked hit me head. So I lost it. Properly, just... I beat her bad. I were hitting and hitting. I didn't know when to stop.

And she were lying there, all bloody. I thought she were dead. And, you know, I wished she were.

CALLUM. Yer mammy?

HARRIET. No, Callum, don't say it like that.

She tries to kiss him. He pulls away.

Say you don't hate us. Come on, man.

Scene Fourteen

The beach. GUSSIE *is on the beach, by the surf. He busily picks up pieces of driftwood and litter and puts them in a pile. When he has finished, he squats next to the pile. He has been beaten up again and now both eyes are blackened. To one side sits the* WOMAN, *grey skin, naked as before, knees up to her chin, lank long hair hanging down.* GUSSIE *flicks the* WOMAN *an occasional glance.* CALLUM *and* HARRIET *cannot see her.*

CALLUM. I'm going home, Gussie. You got the keys?

GUSSIE. I need a light.

CALLUM. What happened to your face, man? More bankers?

GUSSIE. Aye. No.

She's here, Callum.

GUSSIE *picks up some more debris and places it onto the pile.*

She's come. Back to find us.

CALLUM. I'm gettin' our stuff, Gussie. I want us packed up by eight tonight. We're leaving.

GUSSIE *takes the book from his pocket.*

GUSSIE. Remember, fifty-six, thirty-one, twenty-three, nineteen. (*He lays the book down on the pebbles.*) Zero.

CALLUM. Are they in your pocket, Gussie?

GUSSIE. She needs keepin' warm. (*Indicates the pile of driftwood.*) Makin' her a fire, eh.

Pause.

CALLUM. Look at the colour of my nose. Cos o' you, I've been livin' in cold for a week.

GUSSIE. She touched me, Callum.

CALLUM. What?

GUSSIE. Aye!

CALLUM. No way.

GUSSIE. She combed my hair. I touched her skin.

CALLUM. It's yer dreams, man. It doesn't mean it's real.

GUSSIE. Of course. You know best. Just cos you say it isnae true, it isnae true.

CALLUM. This is crazy, wee man. Yer like a ball of string running loose.

GUSSIE. Do you think I am?

CALLUM. You're not. I cannae let ye.

GUSSIE. Aye, cos you're big brother and know better. See this. (*Re: the bin liner.*) This Ma's selkie skin. Remember, without it they cannae change back.

If she's shed her skin, she'll no' change back.

I'm no' lettin' her change back.

Pause.

CALLUM. I've seen her too. Every day. Everywhere. I've seen her on buses, walking up the street. In the dark, in the windows.

You saw her go. You saw her coffin. Remember us carryin' it. Pishin' it down wi' rain. You tripped on the AstroTurf.

Remember it goin' in the ground.

Remember throwin' earth down.

Remember your muddy fingers.

She's buried and she's dead.

Gussie, c'mon. Say it, man. She's dead.

GUSSIE. No' to me, eh? And nor to you too if you were a good son.

CALLUM. Am no' going there.

GUSSIE. Aye, cos you didnae care in the first place.

CALLUM. Wha' ye sayin' this for, Gussie?

GUSSIE. Cos she said, Callum. That you didn't love her. You were always making her feel guilty for going out wi' her mates. All she wanted was a few drinks.

CALLUM. Never just a few drinks.

GUSSIE. Liked a laugh.

CALLUM. Never with us.

GUSSIE. Cos you were always round yer mates'.

The WOMAN *walks into the sea. As the* WOMAN *goes under the waves,* HARRIET *enters.*

CALLUM. And you know why, wee man, cos I used to hate it, aged ten, midnight, me under my duvet, the sound of the latch, the tread of the steps, the door creak. Then the stumble, always the stumble before the drop of weight and the patting hands and vinegar breath and vinegar kisses.

GUSSIE. She loved ye.

CALLUM. Am no' saying I didn't…

GUSSIE. But what?

GUSSIE *notices that the* WOMAN *has entered the sea.*

CALLUM. I shouldnae have been left makin' yer pieces and takin' ye to school. Lettin' ye hang on tae my friends. Playing in the same games, wearing the same clothes – always eating into my life.

GUSSIE. Am no' hangin' onto ye now.

CALLUM. And look what's happened.

GUSSIE *takes off the bin liner. He throws it into the sea. He begins undressing.*

What ye daein'?

GUSSIE. I'm goin' in.

CALLUM. It's freezing, ye dick.

GUSSIE. I'll make life easy for you.

HARRIET. Don't do this, man.

GUSSIE. Have him all to yourself, hen. You'd like that?

GUSSIE *steps into the water. After each sentence he takes a step back, deeper into the water.*

You don't need me any more, Callum.

CALLUM. Gussie, stop.

GUSSIE *walks further back, all the while staring straight at* HARRIET.

GUSSIE. She's poisoned ye against me, turned ye against me and Mammy.

HARRIET. I ain't, man.

CALLUM. She hasnae.

GUSSIE. But you do, you love her more than Mammy. More than me.

HARRIET. You don't, Callum?

GUSSIE. Say it. You do.

GUSSIE *takes another step back.*

CALLUM. What if I do?

But she's made my life fun.

GUSSIE. I'm your brother.

CALLUM. I'm yours! Let me have something, at least something. Mammy's dead but at least she fuckin' lived!

HARRIET *approaches. She takes his hands and interlocks her fingers with his.*

GUSSIE. No!

CALLUM *looks up at* HARRIET *and then to* GUSSIE.

It's me or her, man!

GUSSIE *steps further back into the water.* CALLUM *takes steps towards* GUSSIE. *He turns to look at* HARRIET. *He stops walking.*

Come and get me!

No, Callum.

CALLUM *doesn't move.* GUSSIE *shakes his head and steps further back and then turns and dives under the waves and swims.*

CALLUM. Gussie!

GUSSIE *is far out.* CALLUM *begins undressing. He undresses down to his pants.*

HARRIET. Callum, what you doin'?

CALLUM *runs into the surf.*

You'll freeze, man.

CALLUM. I cannae fuckin' swim!

HARRIET. Gussie!

He'll die in there, Callum.

GUSSIE. Callum!

CALLUM. I can't see ya! Come back in.

HARRIET *quickly takes off her shoes and top and prepares to go in.*

HARRIET. You can't let him –

GUSSIE. Out here! I can see her. There are seals. I can see loads of them. Out here.

C'mon!

CALLUM *doesn't know whether to stay with* HARRIET *or swim to* GUSSIE. *He runs in, up to his chest. He stops. He can't see* GUSSIE. GUSSIE *is about twenty-five metres away.* GUSSIE *swims on. He stops. He panics.*

Callum! I cannae... Callum! Help me!

CALLUM. GUSSIE!

Scene Fifteen

GUSSIE *swims out to sea and is engulfed by the waves, he swims, then floats.*

GUSSIE. I couldnae touch the bottom. There wasnae beach any more, just lights behind me and water, freezin' sea around my feet. It was black and splashin' in my face. So cold. It was just so cold, I stopped.

My arms, like lead, my legs, I couldnae feel me legs. All I could hear was my breathin'… I was so far out. I didnae know what tae dae. I went on my back. So cold.

GUSSIE *floats on the surface of the sea. He ebbs with the flow of the waves.*

Lyin' back, I can hear the echo under the surface. My teeth chattering. Seems like ages, bobbing, just bobbing, looking, waiting.

I feel something touch me. Like it's brushed past my leg, like a jellyfish or a shark. I'm prayin' it's one o' they dolphins cancer kids get. Then again, it brushes past and again and again. Then I feel something else. Under my back, I feel little fingers touching. Prodding. I'm so scared. I cannae move. And the little fingers move from down my back to my legs and my feet. Just feelin'. And I'm grabbed, they grab me and I'm dragged under the water. Swallowing my breath. Kickin' and thrashing. I cannae breathe.

Going under and under, down deeper and deeper. Blacker and blacker.

My lungs burst and I open my eyes. I breathe and I can see, I'm floating and looking down, I can see the bottom. I'm so far down I try and touch it.

The seabed cracks, opens up, bathing GUSSIE *in warm red light.*

A crack's opening. And light's coming out. Bright like fire it is. The crack opens and splits. It's like a cave. Seals, I see. Dozens, I see. All warm in there. I'm reaching out tae them. But they're no' looking up. I'm watching, waiting. One of them is… She's looking at me. And I'm looking back. I'm reachin' out. But she's no' movin'. She wants to but she… I cannae get down further. I cannae get down further. Stuck. I'm screamin', 'Mammy, let me in. Mammy. Let me in.' She looks up and shakes her head.

The seabed closes. GUSSIE *floats to the surface of the water.*

Beat. GUSSIE *now sits in NHS pyjamas in a hospital ward, a week later. There is an awkward silence.* CALLUM *stands, facing the window.*

CALLUM. Raining again, wee man. Straight rain it's been for a week. You're better off inside, staying in the ward. Least it's dry. The roof's leaking at home.

CALLUM *takes out a plastic bag of Frosties and throws them onto the bed in front of* GUSSIE. GUSSIE *opens them hungrily and starts eating.*

They no' feedin' ye?

GUSSIE *continues eating.*

Harriet's away now. On the train last night. I wanna go down. I'm gonna set us up wi' everything. Jobs, flat, the lot.

Yer wanna come, Gussie? I'll only go when you're ready.

Pause.

What dae ye want me to say, man?

GUSSIE. You believe me?

CALLUM. That you were in the water for six days? Do you believe ye?

GUSSIE. Aye.

Slight pause.

CALLUM. Can I believe that you believe it?

Is that enough?

GUSSIE *drops his head.* GUSSIE *shakes his head.*

Why?

Look at me. You can feel my hands, man?

Can you feel them?

GUSSIE. You've always had clammy mits.

CALLUM (*wiping his hands*). You're fucking cold.

Feel this? That's real, man. That's what I know. And you know.

And this bed, this is definite.

And the window.

And these sheets.

72

And I'm your brother and that's definite. Aye?

None of that, that's no' changing.

Anything you need I'll do for you.

The thing I can't believe is you no' letting me change. I want to keep seein' Harriet. You gotta allow that. Cos that's the anything you do for me.

Gussie, agreed, please?

GUSSIE. Aye.

CALLUM. And that's me and you.

Me and you.

GUSSIE *nods in acknowledgement and then grabs* CALLUM *tight and hugs him violently, not letting him go. He lets go.*

The End.

A Nick Hern Book

Cotton Wool first published in Great Britain as a paperback original in 2008 by Nick Hern Books Limited, 14 Larden Road, London W3 7ST, in association with Buckle for Dust

Cotton Wool copyright © 2008 Ali Taylor

Ali Taylor has asserted his right to be identified as the author of this work

Cover image: Duncan Cumming
Cover design: Ned Hoste, 2H

Typeset by Nick Hern Books, London
Printed and bound in Great Britain by Biddles, King's Lynn

A CIP catalogue record for this book is available from the British Library

ISBN 978 1 85459 536 2

Mixed Sources

Product group from well-managed forests, controlled sources and recycled wood or fiber

www.fsc.org   Cert no. TT-COC-002303
© 1996 Forest Stewardship Council

FSC